Darkwind Chronicles

Darkwind Chronicles

The First Act

Christopher Cifelli

Darkwind Chronicles

Copyright © 2020 by Christopher Cifelli. All rights reserved.

No part of this publication may be reproduced, stored in a retrieval system or transmitted in any way by any means, electronic, mechanical, photocopy, recording or otherwise without the prior permission of the author except as provided by USA copyright law.

This novel is a work of fiction. Names, descriptions, entities, and incidents included in the story are products of the author's imagination. Any resemblance to actual persons, events, and entities is entirely coincidental.

The opinions expressed by the author are not necessarily those of URLink Print and Media.

1603 Capitol Ave., Suite 310 Cheyenne, Wyoming USA 82001
1-888-980-6523 | admin@urlinkpublishing.com

URLink Print and Media is committed to excellence in the publishing industry.

Book design copyright © 2020 by URLink Print and Media. All rights reserved.

Published in the United States of America

ISBN 978-1-64367-272-4 (Paperback)
ISBN 978-1-64367-271-7 (Digital)

Fiction
12.08.20

PRELUDE

A Legend...

Eons ago there was a mighty dragon god named Aeternum that was the cleanser of worlds. He would spend several billions of light-years in space travelling to individual worlds, cleansing them of all corruption with his sacred fire and allowing life to start anew. However, there was one world Aeternum couldn't fully cleanse. This world was known as Earth, the cesspool of the universe.

Over the eons, the Earth had sustained billions of different life forms of all kinds, microscopic to colossal, and each time, the planet fell into chaos due to a myriad of reasons. But the root cause was always a single organism, a parasite, that managed to resist being cleansed by the sacred fire each time and it would start anew each time.

Eventually, the parasite became self-aware and devised a plan, which was started by unleashing a disease that turned the humanoid races, humans, elves, orcs and trolls, into werebeasts and to make each race squabble against each other, posing as a deity of sorts. This all came to a head when the orcs began to congregate when their shamans received visions of the other races turning on them and slaying their race to ruin. While a few orc clans advised against taking any drastic actions, many others sought to band together, forming the Orcish Horde.

For the past hundred years, the Orcish Horde began to ravage the lands and fought against the other races, who had created the Coalition, composed of humans, elves, the orcs that left or were exiled from the Orcish Horde, werebeasts, trolls, fairies and many other races, to combat and turn the tide. Eventually, it got to the point where Aeternum, who had been resting on Earth at the time, would have to step in. This is where the parasite made its move.

The parasite infected Aeternum in his tired state and slowly began to drive the dragon god mad as he struggled for control. At the climax of the Orcish Horde's reign, Aeternum, in his maddened state, devastated both the Orcish Horde and the Coalition severely. The dragon god tried to fight back for control, but the parasite's will was too great and eventually, the dragon sacrificed himself by causing an explosion, killing the parasite and members of every race present on the battlefield in the process.

This calm, however, was short lived as the parasite's influence spread across the globe like a plague, infecting many and driving them to madness, sparking the flames of another war, destroying much of the land in the process and splitting the super continent, forcing those who weren't infected to flee.

Eventually, the war turned into a three way stalemate between three remaining kingdoms. Plant, a futuristic kingdom well known for its advanced technology, growing more and more advanced over the years. Stonworth, a medieval kingdom that had military prowess. And Rummi, an elven kingdom that used the environment to their advantage.

Following the destruction of Aeternum led to the creation of a new race, the draconians, or people of the dragon, who rose from his ashes. They've obtained the traits of each race of the Coalition in addition to his own. They were unaffected by the parasite's influence, but were often the target by others in the war. The draconian race, only about thousands strong, couldn't find salvation to the surface world and eventually burrowed underground and went into hiding for the survival of their race.

The constant war had caused the Earth to suffer dearly and landscape to change. Some animals and plants mutated into vile monsters, many of the native races began to dwindle to the point of extinction, and the Earth was on the verge of becoming a wasteland.

When hope seems lost, the draconians, who had spent the past thousand years, had become a formidable race and, a small group of draconians, led by a fairy, had gone further beyond and became the Legendary Dragon Knights. With the war still raging on, the Dragon Knights could not allow it to continue anymore. Eventually, the Dragon Knights found out that the parasite managed to survive and was using the people of Earth to continue it's reign unopposed.

Thanks to their noble deeds, hardships, and sacrifices, the Dragon Knights eventually defeated the parasite, thus sealing it away deep underground, in a holy device called the Devil's Machine. The device's holy properties weaken the parasite's influence and loosen its grip on the natives. Earth began to rebuild.

However, while the parasite was weakened, its rage didn't, and it vowed to return. Plotting for its freedom.

Introduction Saga

EPISODE 1

The beginning of a journey

Standing on the top of a hill within a deep forest was a male draconian. He had orange hair, blue eyes, pale skin, an average, muscular build and a prehensile tail that was the length of a limb. He wore commoner clothing, complete with a shirt and pants, and a pair of shoes. This was Magnetin Darkwind, and he held a sword in his hand. At full height, he stands at five foot ten.

The area Magnetin was standing in was his private training spot, one of the trees was completely bare of leaves, which Magnetin used to practice his sword training on. This tree had a black crow perched on one of the branches, looking at Magnetin from afar.

As Magnetin tries to figure out what happened, a voice calls him. "MAGNETIN!"

Magnetin turned to see a tiny, orange-scaled dragon fly towards him. This was Kamori.

"Oh, hey, Kamori!" Magnetin greeted his companion.

"What do you mean, 'Oh, hey, Kamori'? I've been flying for an hour looking for you."

"I was here all along. Training, you should know that."

"Yeah, well, whatever. Blue girl has been calling for you to help out with lunch."

"It's lunch time already? Oh man… First, I trained, then I was reminiscing…"

"Wait! You mean you are training while reminiscing!" Kamori sounded scared before slowly moving away from him. "Damn, you're nuts!"

"Please, I've trained in my sleep."

"Well, at any rate, Blue girl wants you to help with cooking."

"Fish, again? That's the fifth time this week."

"You know Blue girl doesn't like meat."

"But I'm getting sick of fish…" Magnetin said with a sigh. "Alright, once more then I'm getting some steak in the city."

"You can definitely count me in. I'm itching for some meat myself."

Magnetin chuckles at this. He and Kamori made their way down the trail to his house, it was a haven for him to get away from city life.

Sitting by a campfire, preparing lunch, was a woman. She had long blue hair, yellow eyes, fair skin, a curvaceous build with a big bust, and her ears were pointing outward. She wore clothing fit for an acolyte. This is Delphine Lightwind, and she had a mace strapped to her belt. At her full height, she stands at a whopping seven feet.

The house itself was slightly outside of the forest with several trees scattered throughout the plot with a river just a few meters away. This was the kind of peace Magnetin liked.

Magnetin just looked and walked towards Delphine, who was waiting for him.

"There you are, Magnetin!" She waved at him. "I need some help with some logs for the firewood. Can you get some wood for me?"

"Sure thing!" He looked at the spot in front of Delphine before snapping his fingers and a bonfire appeared at the very spot. "Being a fire draconian is so convenient."

"That works, too. Thank you!" Delphine said, so eager to cook as she took the recently caught fishes and put them in the frying pan. Magnetin sits down on the stump on the opposing side of the bonfire from Delphine.

"So have you heard the news today?"

"About the earthquake? Actually, yes I have. It opened up a cave in the mountains. So what are you planning to do?"

"Well, Andrew and Andrea are going to go explore and they asked me to come along."

"What do you think is--?" Delphine stopped herself as she heard the fishes sizzling and quickly turned them. "--In there!!"

"I don't know, but Andrew and Andrea want to find treasure."

"Well, we can adventure later. Let's eat!" Magnetin, Delphine, and Kamori took a bit of their own fish.

"So, why exactly are they asking you to come along?" Delphine asked as she ate some of her fish.

"Something to do with their father not letting them go alone, I didn't get the full details," Magnetin said. "And that's why the twins want me to go with them,

"Be careful, alright," Delphine cautioned.

"I'll be just fine. I don't think anyone around there will take me out." Magnetin said. "But you can come along as well if you're concerned."

"I probably should," Delphine nodded after taking a moment to consider. "The twins can get a bit reckless sometimes."

The three got up and walked over to the house and gathered some items and took their leave for Oceanus City. Looking from a distance, a robot was hiding in the forest.

"Life form data... Located targets..." The robot said.

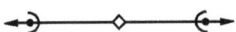

The three hurried along the forest path to Oceanus City. The forest was big and filled with lots of trees that could make the inexperienced traveler lose their way and along the way, they notice the monster activity has steadily increased but wasn't much of a challenge for them. The monsters were the usual giant bees, mushrooms, and the slimes. But they were more numerous which may still prove dangerous for some travelers.

"Okay," Magnetin said, "how many monsters have we slain thus far?"

"25 by my count," Kamori replied.

"Maybe the recent earthquake has made the monsters here restless." Magnetin thought out loud.

"I hope that's the only cause," Delphine muttered. They followed the path until they came up to the river.

"We should be at Oceanus City soon," Magnetin said as he sees the river. "We just need to follow the river until we get to the bridge. That's where we turn." They continued forward, fighting a few more groups of monsters until finally reaching the bridge. They safely made it to Oceanus City. This city was given that name because it's built near the ocean and is one of the three main trade cities of the world, they have docks and use their ships to make deliveries to the other two major continents, and one of the busiest. Delphine has a house here as well as a church which she attended to until it got destroyed by an earthquake a few weeks ago. Likely for her, she wasn't near it at the time, but her adopted father was.

The people here always help one another, but it wasn't like that before as there were some people that were up to no good in the past, but once Magnetin came around, that stopped. The city wasn't as busy with the recent earthquakes but was still lively. The two headed over to the Cashit Shop, that was until Delphine bumped into someone.

He was a male orc. He had long black hair in a mullet style with a beard, black eyes, dark orange skin and a muscular build. He wore an aquamarine sleeveless vest which exposed his ripped arms covered with tattoos of anchors and seagulls, with matching jeans, an orange-white stripe undershirt, a pair of black shoes and had some rope wrapped around his waist. This was Cinghiale, and he had appeared to be drinking a little too much.

"I'm sorry, sir," Delphine apologized.

"Get outta the way, girlie," the drunken Cinghiale said rudely, slurring his words. This orc stood at seven feet.

"Hey, back up, orc," Magnetin advised. "You're too drunk to be walking around by yourself."

"Who asked you, lizard!?" Cinghiale yelled in his drunken anger as he took a swing at Magnetin, who easily ducked the blow, drew his sword and slashed the side of the orc's left arm before holding the tip of the blade up to the orc's neck.

Oh, shit! You're Magnetin Darkwind!? Cinghiale thought as he snapped out of his drunken stupor. Magnetin grabbed the orc's vest collar and pulled him down to his level.

"First and foremost, and I'm going to tell you once, I'm not a lizard! I am a draconian! And second, unless you want to be turned into a smoldering mess, I suggest you run! Is that understood?" Magnetin threatened. He doesn't like being called a lizard.

"U-understood!" The spooked orc shivered.

"Now get outta here." Cinghiale turned and ran as if his life depended on it. Magnetin sheath his weapon. "Are you okay, Del?"

"I'm alright."

"Sorry, you had to see that Del."

"Oh, that's quite alright! Besides, you let him off easy. He wouldn't want what I had in mind."

The group hurried over until they reached the Cashonit Shop. This is one of the successful businesses in the entire Oceanus City, they sell things from weapons to armor to necessities. As they got to the store…

"I said: No, You're not going!" A male voice was heard from within.

"But there could be some treasure in that cave and some other stuff," A boy's voice was heard.

"I don't care, you're not going to that place."

"Uh-oh!" Magnetin hurries in as he quickly evaded an incoming vase. "Whoa!" Delphine hurried inside as well.

Within the shop, the duo saw the store owner arguing with his children about entering a cave for their own safety. The store attendants were a little scared at their boss's outburst.

Standing in the center of the room was a middle-aged man. He had balding, brown hair with several grays, black eyes, pale skin and a slightly rotund build due to his success as a businessman. He wore a white shirt with trousers and a gray necktie. This was Mr. Cashonit. He stood at five foot eleven.

Standing in front of him were his two children. The first was a young man. He had blonde hair, yellow eyes, pale skin and an average build. He wore a coat, jeans, shoes, gloves, a belt with pouches, vials and flasks, and a garment that went down to his calves. This was Andrew Cashonit, and he had a one-handed axe strapped to his belt.

Next to Andrew was a young woman, his fraternal twin sister. She had medium length brown hair tied up in a ponytail, purple eyes, slightly tanned skin and a well-toned build due to her profession with a large bust. She wore a white zipped up vest that showed her midriff, with a pair of denim jeans, arm guards, gloves and boots. This was Andrea Cashonit, and she had a warhammer strapped to her back.

Together, they were known as the Cashonit twins, and they both stood at five foot five.

"The recent earthquakes caused an avalanche to block the road leading to the forest and made the monsters in that area more active! On top of that, there's a rumor that a big tree monster that guards the forest has woken up and has become aggressive!" Mr. Cashonit shouted.

"We know the risks, but we won't know what's inside that cave. Plus there might be others trying to go there as well," Andrew explained. Andrew the more logical one of the Cashonit Twins, he's also more knowledgeable in medicine, potions, and elixirs.

"No one would be foolish enough to go in there."

"That's because no one is good friends with Magnetin, like us," Andrea stated. Andrea was the more determined one of the Cashonit Twins, she is interested in materials and making powerful weapons and armor for travelers. Andrew's logic and Andrea's determination made them a great team.

"Magnetin Darkwind!?" Mr. Cashonit was shocked to hear that. "You've asked him to help you?"

"Yes," Andrew replied, looking behind, "as a matter of fact, he's here."

Mr. Cashonit looks over to see Magnetin near the door entrance.

"Hey, took you long enough," Andrea looked relieved.

"Sorry about that," Magnetin apologized, "monsters are more of a hassle than I thought."

"See, dad?" Andrew said, "we'll be safe as long as Magnetin keeps the monsters at bay."

"Even if, Magnetin helps you," Mr. Cashonit reminded, "you still have the avalanche of boulders to take care of."

"I think Anita would have something to deal with that?" Delphine asked.

"Don't worry, Mr. Cashonit. If anything those monsters do try anything, they are as good as dead," Magnetin assured.

Mr. Cashonit turns around. "Go… But don't say, I didn't warn you."

"Father?"

"And a little-known advice: Don't let greed consume you, it'll be your undoing," he turns his head slightly back, "Kids…" Cashonit heads to the back of the store and slams the door behind him.

"Thanks for showing up when you did," Andrew said, showing a sigh of relief.

"Is your father okay with this? Those monsters are more challenging in groups," Magnetin said, looking concerned.

"Now that that's out of the way. Let's meet up with Anita," Andrea interjected. Magnetin shrugged as they weren't listening.

"She should be at her store," Delphine stated.

"Alright, let's go!"

The team began to hurry over to Anita's Engineering shop, bringing the twin's merchant cart along. Anita was well known for her engineering skills and intelligence. But she wasn't there instead, there was a note left on her door, stating that she has left for the time being. Magnetin was able to pick up Anita's scent which directed him towards the direction of the rock slide. With that in mind, Magnetin's team headed out and left Oceanus City. The monster activity had simmered down a bit but was still a bit dreadful for travelers. The team took this opportunity and quickly through the area.

At the entrance of the forest was a female elf with red hair, emerald green eyes and a slim figure with an average bust. She wore a pair of aviator glasses, a black jacket with a matching pair of jeans over a purple tube top, black cowgirl boots and diamond shaped earrings that had the infinity symbol engraved in them. This was

Anita Lastum, and in the holster on her belt was a heavily modified pistol with a silver finish and a golden handle with the name "Jesse" engraved on the barrel, along with a sheathed combat dagger and several grenades. She was seen blowing bubblegum.

"Well, y'all sure took your sweet time," Anita said with her southern accent after popping her bubble.

"Yeah, well, you're the only one in Oceanus City that knows how to make the best bombs," Magnetin said.

"The only ones in the world!" Anita proudly said. "Out of household chemicals, thank you very much."

"The rock slide shouldn't be too far, just have to watch out for monsters," Delphine explained.

"While I plant it, y'all will have to cover me," Anita reminded.

"I can't wait for all the good weapons and armor to make from the ore from that cave." Andrea was getting excited.

"Remember what Dad said: Don't be consumed by greed," Andrew reminded her.

"I'm not trying to be greedy. I'm just excited."

"Alright, everyone ready?" Delphine announced.

The team headed deeper into the forest, with Magnetin leading the way while Anita covered the back.

EPISODE 2

Legends of the Past

The deeper they went, the thicker and bigger the trees got as they traveled through the forest, fending off any monsters that came close to the group, they made their way to the rock slide. A large dam of boulders was blocking the path. Climbing it didn't seem like the best of ideas. Anita placed her bag down and took out some stuff.

"This will only take a moment," Anita informed.

"What stuff did you bring?" Delphine asked.

"Just some explosives this will help clear the boulders," Anita said, as she placed the explosives onto the boulders, in between several cracks where it would be most effective, and took out the timer attached to her belt. "Okay! Get back!" She then set the timer for 30 seconds and hurried over to the group as they duck for cover, using the cart as a shield. An explosion follows shortly afterward as rocks and debris flew past them. As the smoke cleared, Anita looked to the landslide. It has been completely destroyed.

"Man, what was in those things?" Magnetin said.

"Household chemicals in the proper proportion are wired with plastic explosives," Anita replied.

"That clears this road bump," Magnetin said, "Now all that's left is that tree monster."

"There should be a cave along the mountain's base, which leads into the mountain. There should be loads of treasure inside," Andrew replied. The group paced themselves and hurried along the road to the base of the mountain, the trees covered most of it aside from the grassy path in front of them. "I don't see a cave?" Andrew said.

"That's odd the cave was reported to be here…" Andrea stated.

"No harm in looking around then," Anita replied. The group spread out to explore the mountain base, not much to look at as the trees that block most of the walkway, except for Magnetin himself, who stood still as he detected a familiar presence coming from within the mountain.

"There's something in there…" Magnetin said to himself. Kamori landed on Magnetin's head as he looked towards the mountain.

"I feel something, too…" Kamori said. Magnetin walked forward to the mountain base and looked at the rock formation on how it's shaped. It looked way too smooth.

"This looks like… a door…" Magnetin replied as he feels around for a switch or something. Delphine decided to sit on a small boulder for a bit as she was tired from the walk and the battles. The moment she did, she felt as if the boulder began to sink slowly into the ground. As the boulder sank, the door opened up as if it were by magic. "Hey, the door opened up! Nice work, Del." Magnetin looks towards her as she gave a thumbs up.

"Don't mention it," Delphine replied. The group gathered around the entrance.

"Shall we?" Magnetin said as he stepped inside. His friends all followed him.

"A great treasure awaits us, sis!" Andrew said.

"Let's get what we came for!" Andrea replied.

"I thought it would be fun and challenging. But I haven't even shot one bullet yet," Anita said.

"Don't get cocky, Anita," Delphine warned her friend.

In the forest, a creature was watching them. As the group travels farther into the cave to see the area slowly change as the walls, ceiling, and floor from being rocky to as smooth as crystal, in fact, the area was made of crystals. Most of the area showed their reflection, which made it almost confusing to traverse through. There was a sign on the wall that had some odd writing.

"What's this writing?" Anita said.

"I can't recognize it myself," Delphine said.

"It's in Draconic," Magnetin said.

"You can translate it?" Anita asked.

"Yes," Magnetin replied as he read the sign. "'For the ones who represent an essence of eternity will find the way where only the fey thread and find what they're seeking. But beware--'"

"Beware what?"

"That's all I can say after reading this. The rest of the message appears to be illegible," Magnetin stated.

"So it states, 'For those who represent an essence of eternity.' What does that mean?" Anita said. Everyone, but Kamori, shook their heads.

"Eternity?" Kamori said to himself.

"You're actually thinking, Kamori? Heh, that's a first," Magnetin jokes.

"Hey, I can think!" Kamori growled.

"'Essence.'" Anita continued.

"Oh, it's referring to the Essences of Aeternum, the dragon god!" Delphine exclaimed as it came to her. "Since his destruction, Aeternum's essences had split across the globe. The draconians, who are the descendants of Aeternum, are said to house at least one of his essences within them. Aspect of Eternity is a religion based on it, which I so happen to follow."

"Makes sense, Delphine," Magnetin said. "Each draconian has an element that is tied to an essence. I'm a fire draconian so my essence would be the Heart."

"So you have the heart of an actual god?" Andrea asked.

"You can say that," Magnetin said as he turned to the path forward and felt a strong presence leading him throughout the cave. Delphine caught wind of this.

"Magnetin, where are you going?" Delphine said.

"I can feel something… from deeper in this cave…" Magnetin said.

"Wait up!" Delphine said, chasing after him.

"Del! Wait up!" Anita calls out as the group hurries to catch up to Delphine. Magnetin continues on traveling the cave until he comes to what appears to be a dead end. There is a door made out of crystal-like the rest of the cave, it blends in well, but Magnetin can see it. Delphine catches up with him, panting.

"W-wait… Up…" Delphine heaved.

"This is the entrance," Magnetin said. He could hear a voice calling him. *…How…the…pow…er…*

"Huh?" Delphine regains her posture. She looks around and finds no door. "But, there's no door."

…Heart… show… the… power… and open… the way… Magnetin keeps on hearing the same line over. He holds his hands in front of him and begins to channel his draconic powers.

"Magnetin?" Delphine said.

"Quiet, blue girl!" Kamori said to her, before looking over to Magnetin again. "Magnetin is concentrating on opening the path."

"How do you know this stuff, Kamori?" Delphine asked him. Kamori didn't answer, just looked at Magnetin.

Heart. Show the power, and open the way.

"Hellfire!" Magnetin called out, as a barrage of fireballs shot out of his hands and rapidly hit the crystal door. The rest of the group managed to see him a moment before the attack was called. The crystal began to melt away, revealing a metal door. Magnetin stopped after a few minutes, panting from overuse of his power, but regained his posture quickly.

"There is a door," Delphine said to herself in amazement, before looking at Magnetin.

"Draconians are something else," Anita said with an impressed tone.

Magnetin approaches the metal door grabs the handle and began to pull it open. It was hard as the doors were too heavy for even his draconic strength. "What's this door made of?" Magnetin began to feel that someone else was pulling as well. It was Delphine, Anita, Andrew and Andrea, which gave Magnetin a smile. A crack was heard as they continue. "Keep it up!" Kamori shouted, cheered them on.

"One more!" With one mighty pull, the door finally opened up. The recoil caused them to lose balance.

"Is everyone okay?" Magnetin said.

"We're fine, thanks," Delphine replied.

"Speak for yourself," Andrew grumbled.

As they enter through the doorway, the group awed at a marvelous area they have ever set eyes on. The entire area was covered by beautiful crystals. Just then, a hooded figure appeared before them, he was donned in sage robes.

"Welcome…" The figure said.

In the crystal cave, the hooded being that appeared before they began to approach them. "It has been centuries since we have had visitors from the outside world. My name is Shendu, the Gatekeeper." He removes his hood to reveal that his head resembles a Chinese dragon while his hands looked like dragon claws.

"Where are we?" Magnetin asked.

"A sacred place where only draconian and fairies can tread," Shendu said. "Can I ask for your names?"

"I'm Magnetin Darkwind."

"Darkwind?" Shendu said, raising a brow, "you wouldn't happen to know someone named Seth Darkwind?"

"Seth Darkwind? Never heard of that person."

"I see…" Shendu replied.

"I'm Delphine Lightwind," the acolyte replied.

"Anita Lastum. I'm a good friend."

"Andrew Cashonit! An aspiring alchemist!"

"Andrea Cashonit! An aspiring blacksmith!"

"And we're the Cashonit Twins!" The twins announced in unison. Kamori just shook his head.

"Follow me, we have much to talk about. Your destiny lies at the end of this tunnel," Shendu said, walking down the path. Magnetin followed closely at his side. "If you're able to open the door, then one of you must have one of the essences of Aeternum, the dragon god."

"That'd be me," Magnetin asked. "I am a fire draconian, so my essence would be the Heart, correct?"

"Yes! The Heart is one of eight essences of Aeternum and it is tied to the element of fire." Shendu said as he went on. "As a gatekeeper, it's my duty to prevent those who would seek harm to our kind while welcoming those with the right power. I've guarded this door for centuries waiting for someone of your caliber."

Somehow, I don't think that's true... the dubious Anita thought to herself.

"What's down this tunnel?" Magnetin asked.

"You'll see, young whelp," Shendu said to the young warrior. This caused Magnetin to stop and wonder what he meant by that statement. The group noticed several female humanoids with wings hiding between the rocks and crystals. The shape of these wings varies from birds to reptiles to insects.

"Those are fairies, right?" Andrea whispered to Delphine.

"I believe so," Delphine replied. "We must be near a fairy fountain then…"

"A simple treasure hunt just turned into something interesting…" Anita muttered.

They continued until they reached a long bridge leading to another crystal cave at the end. The gap was very deep and dark with no signs of seeing the bottom.

"You may want to be careful though… Or you can spend the rest of your life falling for eternity." Shendu cautioned. This struck fear into Anita and the Cashonit Twins. Magnetin and Delphine continued but stopped when they saw their friends petrified.

"What's wrong, though I already know the answer." An unsurprised Magnetin said.

"Come on, Anita," Delphine said to her friend, "it's only 30 or so feet away."

"Is it secured at least?" Anita asked.

"Well, we're on it," Magnetin said, "I say it's secure enough."

"That's true, but…" Anita was still frightened.

"How about one of us walked with --Ah!?" Magnetin said but got interrupted as Anita rushed over to grab Magnetin's arm.

"Don't let me fall!" Anita shouted, tightening her grip as her voice echoed through the abyss. Magnetin started to walk slowly, with Anita in tow.

"You two coming?" Delphine asked the twins as she began to cross. Andrew and Andrea were having problems mustering the courage.

"I'm having second thoughts, Andrew," Andrea said to her brother. Her fear was overpowering her determination as she slowly backed away from the bridge.

"But there is a treasure on the other side…" Andrew said, trying not to lose his cool.

"What's the point of treasure if we're dead?!" Andrea asked.

"D-don't say stuff like that!" Andrew replied, trying to keep his sister from freaking both of them out. "We gotta give it a chance. We won't be able to face our father if all we do is just cower at every single obstacle in our path."

"Al-alright…" Andrea agreed as the Cashit Twins slowly crossed the bridge. Magnetin and Anita already made it safely across.

"You can open your eyes, Anita. We made it across," Magnetin said as Anita slowly saw the crystal cavern. She lets out a sigh of relief. "You can let go now." Anita blushed as she realizes that she was still clinging to Magnetin's arm and quickly let go.

"We're safe," Delphine said to the twins, who let out a sigh of relief. The group continued to follow Shendu until they reached a chamber with a large stone tablet. In front of it lies an orb held the claw of a statue of a dragon.

"This…isn't one of those fairy fountains, right?" Anita asked Delphine.

"No, this area's too small for something like that," Delphine responded.

"This orb contains the power of Aeternum. No mere mortal can obtain it," Shendu explained. "This mural explains the conflict between the dragon god and the parasite."

"Yes, being an acolyte of the Aspect of Eternity, I know of that conflict well," Delphine with a nod. "It's what led to the creation of the draconians as well as the religion."

"This is all boring to me…" Andrea said with a yawn.

The gatekeeper turned to Delphine, "while that was an important piece of history, what you know about that conflict it wasn't entirely true. However, that's a tale for another time." He turned back to Magnetin. "Now. Magnetin Darkwind, this orb has waited for you to come along, as it is now time for your trial. But be warned, once you accept this, there will be no turning back.

"Also, do be careful, for once you have this power, there will be others who will try to take it from you for their own selfish gain. Be on your guard and face each challenge as they arise whilst under your own judgment. Now, absorb the orb and your trial shall begin."

Magnetin began to walk toward the statue but turned to his friends. "Should I?"

"Go ahead, Magnetin!" Delphine said, with a smile on her face. "If anyone can do it, it's you! Believe in yourself!"

Magnetin continued walking toward the statue, stood in front of the orb being held out and slowly placed his hand on it. A stream of energy began siphoning from the orb. Magnetin couldn't remove his hand as the orb was fully absorbed into his being. "Wha…?" Nothing happened. A gold pendant had appeared around Magnetin's neck.

"It is done. That pendant now symbolizes your transitioning to becoming a Dragon Knight Trainee and is required that you keep it around your neck. This is only the beginning, whelp," Shendu stated, "for now your trail begins."

"I'll accept it," Magnetin nodded, "where do I need to go?"

"I'll mark their locations on your map. Once you're done, you'll become a Dragon Knight. Then the orb will manifest."

"I guess we'll head back to Oceanus City for now."

"Wait," Andrea said. "We came here to look for some treasure. You know, gold, diamonds, crystals."

"…………………" Shendu walked over to a wall and tossed over a crystal to Andrew. He looked apprehensive to touch it at first.

"Finally! Now, dad can get off our backs!" Andrew and Andrea left the cavern, all delighted.

"Just between us, why are humans so interested in dragon turd?" Shendu asked.

"Eww…" Delphine and Anita said, squinting their eyes in disgust. Kamori couldn't help but laugh. Several mischievous giggles from the fairies could also be heard.

Somethings never change… Magnetin thought with a groan at the fairies being mischievous as always.

And with that, the Magnetin's group said their goodbyes to Shendu before they made their way out of the cavern back into the real world. The sun was beginning to set below the horizon.

"Strange, I don't feel any different than how I normally feel," Magnetin stated.

"GUYS!" Andrea called out. They saw a tree monster blocking the way and began roaring in rage.

"This must be what Mr. Cashonit was saying," Delphine pondered.

"Heh, firewood," Magnetin grinned. The battle was on against the tree monster. It started off with Magnetin using Hellfire to scorch the giant plant monster, it countered by swinging its vines violently to deflect the fireballs, with only a few getting through. He then charged forward, moved to the side and slashed it in the trunk. The tree monster's roots grabbed Magnetin's feet and made him fall over, he tried to use his sword to free himself, but the tree monster took the sword from his grasp and threw it just a few feet away, landing beside Anita's feet. She started shooting the tree monster, they effectively pierced through the bark, but they didn't go all the way through. She slowly made her way over to Magnetin's sword. Delphine kept everyone alive and provided beneficial spells, while occasionally damaging their foe.

"Hungry!?" Andrew exclaimed as he threw a vial of alchemical fire at the tree monster. "Eat this!" The alchemical fire shattered and it spewed fire all around the roots, this caused the tree monster to reel back in pain, giving Andrea ample opportunity to strike away at its roots with her warhammer.

"Olly olly oxen free!" Andrea exclaimed as she whacked at the bark of the tree monster's roots.

All of this gave Anita enough time to throw Magnetin's sword to him, who was freed thanks to Andrea whacking at the roots. As the fight went on, the tree monster began to get more trigger happy with its attacks.

"Alright, we need to end this now!" Anita injected.

"Yes! I'm going to be out of mana soon!" Delphine added.

"Let's get serious!" Magnetin cried out subconsciously, branding his new weapon as an aura began to surround him. Andrea, with all her might, swung her warhammer, striking the tree monster's side while Magnetin charged. He slashed through the area Andrea had struck the tree monster at once and nothing happened for a moment until the tree monster suddenly burst into flames as it slowly turned into ash and charcoal. He then, with a snap of his fingers, made the flames vanish without a trace before they could burn the forest. Everyone was in complete amazement at this.

"Whoa, how did that happen?" Magnetin was stumped on how he defeated the tree monster so easily as he looked at his hands.

"That, whelp, was just the beginning. Let's head back home!" Kamori said, jumping on Magnetin's shoulder.

"Yeah!"

On the way back, Andrew said to Andrea: "By the way, 'olly olly oxen free' is a catchphrase for children games, not for warhammer swings."

"Whatever, Mister Know-It-All," Andrea retorted.

From afar, three people were watching the battle on a cliffside, they were werebeasts.

The first was a gray-haired werewolf. He had gray, coursed hair tied in a ponytail, yellow eyes, pale skin, wolf ears, a wolf tail with gray fur and an average, but muscular build. He wore a torn jean jacket, ragged shirt and torn jeans. This was Francis McWolfwood. He stood at five foot eleven.

The second was a bluish gray-haired werecat. She had bluish gray hair tied in a ponytail with a white ribbon, green eyes, pale skin, cat ears, a cat tail with blue fur and a white tip, and a tall, slim build with an average bust. She wore a baggy shirt, a pair of jeans and shoes. This was Lauren Tomcat. She stood at six foot two.

The third was a brown-haired wererat. She had light brown hair in a bob cut, black eyes, fair skin, mouse ears, a brown mouse tail, and a short, curvy build with a large bust. She wore a tank top, a black skirt and high heels. This was Carrie Fieldmouse. She stood at five foot six.

"I can't believe that the tree monster lost to that lizard!" Francis growled, angry that Magnetin's group defeated the tree monster with ease.

"Francis, that tree monster wouldn't have won against them. It's five against one and you know Magnetin's packing fire spells," Carrie stated. "And he's a draconian, not a werebeast like us." The werewolf just huffed in response.

"You know what I think?" Lauren said, lying on her back.

"What, Lauren?" The wererat asked, in a disinterested tone.

"I think that somehow Magnetin's exploration inside the cave has made him stronger."

"We can't rule out that possibility," Carrie said. "But there's no way he'd become that stronger in such a short amount of time."

"I say, that is so crazy, it is nothing but a bunch of baloney!" Francis shouted at the werecat.

"Me-ow!" Lauren shivered in response.

"Alright, you two, that's enough," Carrie said, trying to keep the peace within the group. She looks to see another "Magnetin" looking at Magnetin's group from a distance. "Since when did Magnetin have a twin?"

"Never. He just cloned himself just to spite us. Now, come on. We gotta think of another plan."

Back with the main group.

"Alright, now that we're back in town, let's surprise dad with our treasure," Andrew said with pride in his voice, as the two marched home. Anita tried her best not to think about the crystal.

"I'm beginning to understand why miners always clean their hands before and after mining," Delphine muttered to herself as she looked at Magnetin and wondered if he…

"What?" Magnetin asked. But the look on Delphine's face says it all. "Oh, come on! Draconians don't even defecate! And even if we did, what difference would it make!?"

"Please! Stop talking about that!" Anita begged as she was clearly cringing in disgust.

Kamori needs to stop this. "Alright, alright, you whelps, break it up. Why don't we head home then? It's getting late."

"Magnetin, you can sleep in my house tonight, you haven't done so in years." Delphine offered. And with that, Magnetin followed Delphine home as Anita went back to her shop to stock up on things and prepare herself.

In Delphine's house, Magnetin sat down on the couch as Delphine made dinner for them. Kamori lies down on a cushion.

"Magnetin, do you really want to go on this trial?" Delphine asked, with concern in her voice.

"I don't know, but Shendu was really adamant about it," Magnetin replied, "so I'll do it."

"Where is the closest place for you to go?"

Magnetin looks at the map, "the nearest place should be just south of here, in a desert. The guardian of the earth should be there."

"When are you leaving?"

"I don't know yet. I don't know who I should take with me? Or should I go it alone? Or are you coming along with me?" Magnetin asked as he looked at her.

"You're asking me to come with you? I don't know if I never traveled that far before."

"We can take Anita as well. So, what's for dinner tonight?" Magnetin asked.

"Please, it better not be fish this time," Kamori groaned.

"And what is wrong with fish?"

"What's right with fish?" The two then began to argue with Magnetin used his prehensile tail to grab a pair of ear mufflers and placed them on his ears to drown them out.

Meanwhile, in Anita's workshop, Anita finished making her latest invention: The Microcapsules. She tested it with many objects around the house and now she was testing it on her big wheel truck parked outside her garage.

"This will make traveling easier!" Anita said, putting the final touches and tested it by pressing a button on the driver's side. The big wheel disappeared into a small capsule that could fit in the palm of her hand. "I've finally done it! Now to see if it's in top shape." She pressed a button as she set it back down and backed up. The big wheel re-appeared completely unscathed. "Ha-ha! Another scientific and engineering success! My mama and papa would be proud! If they…" She shook her head, turned her truck back into its capsule containment and placed it on her table. She then had dinner and went to bed shortly after.

Earth and Heavens Saga

EPISODE 3

Guardian of Earth

The next morning, a murder of crows were seen flying at the city's entrance where everyone, minus Andrew and Andrea, met up to prepare for the long journey ahead. Anita's truck was parked on the outskirts of town. The group made sure to wear lighter clothing since they were going into a desert, it's bound to be hot, especially since it's the Searing Desert. Magnetin, however, didn't have to worry about the heat, due to him being a draconian, a fire draconian, no less.

"Everyone is all accounted for?" Magnetin announced.

"I got the first aid kit and brought some food from home, who knows when we'll reach the next town," Delphine smiled.

"I'm all stocked up on ammo, explosives, and the works," Anita said.

"I thought your earring provided you infinite ammo?" Delphine asked.

"They do, but they only work half of the time for specialized ammo and explosives," Anita stated.

"Looks like everything is ready," Kamori said.

"So, did anyone hear about Andrew and Andrea?"

"Here they come." They were pulling their cart with them, not much was in it.

"We're here," Andrew announced.

"There's bound to be places where valuable materials are just waiting for us to come and take it," Andrea spoke, getting excited.

"So a group of 5 people plus one?" Kamori said. "This should be fun."

"Alright, let's move out!" Magnetin command. And with that, they left Oceanus City and followed the road to the south away from the mountain. "The destination we are heading towards is a desert town called Stone Crow Town. The Guardian of Earth lives in that area."

"Let's go then," Delphine said. After attaching the carts to the truck, they were off. Anita was driving the truck as Delphine sat up front with her. The others rode in the back. The ride was nice and relaxing since they'll need it for the journey ahead. The group mainly passed around idle chat as time went on. Eventually, they entered the Searing Desert, they weren't lying about it being hot.

"Searing Desert… What was once a luscious forest has turned into a scorching desert… Hence its name…" Delphine was trying to fan herself. "Whew… People think that we're hot? This desert is hotter."

"We shouldn't have worn bold colors in a desert…" Anita groaned. She had already removed her jacket, revealing her tank top.

"Whew… We probably should have packed more water," Andrea spoke, whipping her head of sweat.

"Least we aren't walking in it," Andrew pointed out.

Shame I'm not old enough to make them dragonborns, Magnetin thought to himself as both he and Kamori were fine in the desert. **But it would have taken too long…**

"Just keep heading south from here and we'll come across the town," Delphine instructed as she looked at the map.

"You got it! Yee-haw!" Anita said with excitement as she honked the horn in tandem. Along the way they saw a muscular humanoid walking along the road, he appeared to be waving at them. By a tree they passed, they saw a flock of vultures feasting on the carcass of a stray cattle.

"Who's that?" Delphine asked. Anita stopped the truck next to the muscular humanoid who approached them.

He was an earth draconian. He had messy brown hair, brown eyes, tan skin and a stubby tail. He wore light clothing, despite not needing to. This was Rex, and strapped to his back was a greataxe.

"He's big!" Andrea was amazed at his height.

"He's a draconian," Magnetin stated. "We can grow upwards of eight feet. So, of course he's big." **He's also a wyrm.**

"Where're ya folks heading towards?" Rex, the earth draconian, asked with a deep, western accent.

"We're looking for a place called Stone Crow Town," Delphine replied.

"That's where I'm heading as well. My family lives there," Rex informed them. "I should be able to get there in a couple of days."

"Need a ride?" Magnetin asked.

"You sure we can trust him, Mag?" Andrew asked with a whisper. "He's a draconian, sure, but…"

"If he wants the help," he replied. "But that's really up to Anita."

"Well, I wouldn't mind a ride, son," Rex said with a grin, "if you got the room for someone of my stature."

"This baby should be big enough to hold you," Anita grinned, patting the steering wheel.

"I appreciate it, lass," the muscular draconian said as he climbed into the back, which those riding in the back moved to accommodate the space needed. The truck began to vibrate and groaned a bit due to the weight as he got on. Anita drove off again.

"So what's your name, mister?" Andrea asked, amazed at the draconian's sheer size.

"I'm called Rex because of my size and stature. And who might y'all be?"

"I'm Magnetin Darkwind and this is my companion, Kamori. The one in blue is Delphine Lightwind, and the one driving is Anita Lastum."

"And we're Andrew and Andrea Cashonit!" The Cashonit Twins said in unison.

"Interesting to see such small humanoids such as yourselves out here," Rex said with a chuckle.

"Who are you calling 'small', ya big palooka!?" The Cashonit Twins exclaimed, but the muscular draconian brushed it aside.

"So why are you all heading to Stone Crow Town?" Rex asked.

"We're trying to find--" Andrea was about to speak when she was interrupted when Kamori covered her mouth.

"We're archaeologists traveling to find ancient valuables and discover numerous artifacts," Andrew said, trying to cover up their own plans.

"I see," Rex said. "None of ya look the part, though."

"We prefer to protect ourselves against potential threats when searching for artifacts," Magnetin added. "You never know what will attack us."

"We're almost at the town. Just a few minutes away." Anita said. They eventually pulled up outside the main gates of Stone Crow Town, it was bigger than they expected for a town to be, but nothing compared to Oceanus City. Most of the buildings here were made of stone, and not steel like what Oceanus City was. Delphine and Anita got out of the car while everyone else hopped out of the back. The Cashonit Twins went to unhook their cart before Anita pressed a button on the driver's side to make it vanish into its capsule form. She placed it in a little box and put it in her pocket.

"I must thank y'all. If you need anything, don't hesitate to call," Rex said as he turned around and walked through the main gate, but not before letting out a tiny smirk.

"What should we do for now?" Anita asked.

"Well, first we should ask for information about the Guardian of Earth," Magnetin replied. "And I appreciated that nobody reveals about our journey until the moment is right. The people still don't know about this, so it'll make our enemies harder to find us. And we also don't want to cause an uproar of any sorts."

"True," Delphine agreed. Everyone entered Stone Crow Town and began to ask anything about the Guardian of Earth, but not much luck on that part. Each member got a "Don't know anything about it.", "Sorry, can't help you.", or anything of the sort. Everyone gathered at the inn for lunch.

"How did it go for all of you?" Magnetin asked.

"Nothing."

"Zero."

"So what now?"

"Seems like y'all are stuck in a rut." A voice was heard. The group looked over to find out that it was Rex, who was calling them.

"Rex? How's your family doing?"

"Yes, they're doing very well. You guys aren't, though."

"Think we can ask him, Magnetin?" Delphine asked. "He might be able to help us."

"Well, it's worth a try anyway. Hey, Rex, do you know where the Guardian of Earth is located?" Magnetin asked.

"The Guardian of Earth? Hmm…" Rex pondered. "I may have an idea of where he's located. I can take you there myself."

"Is it far?"

"No, actually it's just a few yards on the north side of town in a cave."

"Let's finish our meal and head out there," Magnetin announced. And with that, the group followed Rex from the town and around and made it to the cave he mentioned. But when they got to the cave, it appears that monsters were inside.

"It appears that this Guardian of Earth knows of your arrival and decided to test your abilities."

"Very well, then. Let's answer his call by letting ourselves in." Magnetin grinned.

"I'll let your lot handle 'em," Rex said.

"You aren't helping?"

"This is your test, not mine."

"You can spectate then." Everyone went in. There were loads of elemental creatures wandering around the cave as the group worked their way through as well as bats and brown mushrooms. Like the previous cave, this cave changed from being rough to having a smooth stone-like structure. This indicated that they were getting closer to the main chamber. After clearing the last of the monsters standing in their way, there was a stone door to greet them at the end of the tunnel.

"We're here," Magnetin said. Rex walked to the stone door and grabbed both handles and opened it. This led them to an underground cavern with falling sand from above.

"I wonder what kind of ore deposits are down here…" Andrea pondered for a moment. Magnetin decides that it was time to reveal the truth.

"Thank for your help, Rex…" Magnetin grinned. "Or should I say, Guardian of Earth." Rex turned his head slightly to the draconian as he grinned. Kamori grinned as he knew as well. Everyone else was surprised.

"So you knew?" Rex said, still keeping his poker face.

"It's quite obvious when you think about it. I mean, your size and stature and the convenience of knowing where we needed to go? Also you being an earth draconian. Dead giveaways."

"Looks like you're smarter than I took you for," Rex said, dropping the western accent. Impressive. But I know why you're here and it isn't for artifacts."

"So we can focus on the task at hand."

"Then follow me." The group followed Rex to a large arena surrounded by quicksand. There appeared to be no spectators, though. Rex walked over as he turned to the group. "I am Rex, the Dragon Knight of the Earth and one of the eight guardians. You passed the first trial with ease, but now we shall get on with the actual test."

"Name it."

"It's simple, really," Rex said as he held an item in his hand, a heart made of stone. "First, you must venture into a maze I have constructed, find this artifact and then return it here. There's no time limit, but the difficulty of the next test will be harder if you take longer than 15 minutes." Rex held the item in his hand before sending it off across the plain and placed it on a pedestal at the end of a stone maze. "As you travel through the maze, there will be traps and monsters placed to block your way. There's also dead ends. On this portion of the test, your friends can help you out, but only one can help." Rex takes a glance at Kamori. "Including your companion, of course. Now choose your allies."

"Who do you want to join you?" Delphine said. Magnetin walked up a cliff and examined the stone maze from a higher altitude, analyzing it and formulating a plan. He sees various monsters along the maze as well as some revealed traps lying in wait. Some of the traps may be hidden. By using his eyes, he made a photographic memory of the layout of the maze and the quickest way to get the item and back. There may also be a chance that the maze might change at any given time.

"I've decided that it'll be me and Anita," Magnetin announced. "Anita can shoot at any monsters from a distance and also disarm any traps."

"Fighting in a maze will be good to practice close quarters combat," Anita figured. She throws a stopwatch to Delphine. "Keep track of the time."

"You're all set? Now, remember, only you can grab the item," Rex announced. "Not your comrade, but she can still help otherwise. Now stand on the starting point." The group did as they were told. As they stepped on it, a barrier surrounded the edge of the starting point. "The only way to drop this barrier is the item."

"No pressure…" Anita said sarcastically.

"Ready? GO!" Rex announced as the group quickly ran into the maze. They took twists and turns as they made their way through. Anita sensed a trap in the floor ahead of them.

"Pitfall into spikes! Jump!" Anita announced. The duo performed a long jump over the trap as the floor crippled. Anita tracked a beast around the corner. "There's a monster around the next corner. A big one!" Anita said. This bull was a true monster. Magnetin ran along the wall, bounced off it and slashed the beast in the head and jumped on its back. Anita branded her revolver and blasted it in the head before kicking it into a wall. Within a few moments, the beast fell. The group pressed on as Magnetin felt the item down the hallway. Anita detected a trap in the wall.

"Stop! Arrows!" She said. The duo came to a halt as Anita searched for a control panel in the wall and deactivate the trap. "GO!" Magnetin continued until they reached the pedestal, the trainee walked up to it and picked up the artifact. Upon grabbing it, the ground vibrated quickly, a roof appeared over the maze itself, shrouding the maze in darkness.

"Good things we can see in the dark, right, Anita?" Magnetin smiled.

"We can only see in grayscale, though," Anita pointed out. "Let's hurry back."

Outside of the maze, Delphine looked at the stopwatch with 6:54 on it and counted down. "Less than 7 minutes left." During this time, Andrew was having a conversation with Rex.

"Hey, so are these trials meant to prove what exactly?" Andrew asked Rex. "We know how strong Magnetin is. So this all seems rather pointless to me."

"While I have no doubt that Magnetin is strong, he's still a whelp," Rex said. "And becoming a Dragon Knight is something that requires him to overcome life's challenges and be the best of the best. And you say it's pointless, but I can say the same about you becoming an alchemist and your sister becoming a blacksmith."

"And just how the hell did you know that!?" Andrea exclaimed. "I don't recall either of us ever telling you our dreams! That's an invasion of privacy!"

"Ha-ha! We all have our secrets," Rex said with a hearty laugh, "don't we, eh!?"

Delphine suddenly heard the sounds of gunshots, scraping metal, and a monster moaning. Out came a blood bathed Magnetin and Anita. Magnetin had the artifact in his blood-covered hand.

"That last monster WAS a real monster." Magnetin smiled, claiming their victory.

"Whew! You both reek of blood!" Delphine held her nose.

"Well done," Rex said to the Dragon Knight trainee. Magnetin hands the artifact. "Maybe I should have set more traps and have more monsters with a bigger maze. Regardless, you have done the task well and now onto the main test: Defeat me."

"Lead the way."

Rex led the group over to the arena and set the stone heart down on a pedestal. Kamori was giving Magnetin some info about Rex.

"Rex may seem big and powerful, but he's slow because of that and he's vulnerable to fire. Use what you have to your advantage. And stock on some potions."

Magnetin grabbed at least three and put them in different pockets. After that he entered the ring with Rex, while wearing powerful armor, though, he was missing a helmet and shoulder pieces. It looked like berserker armor.

"By ending in a short about of time, I haven't got much time to prepare myself. A strategy in war is to attack your foes while they're preparing, this can be used to turn the tide of battle." He grabbed the greataxe on his back. "The condition for victory is whoever is the last one standing. Don't hold back on my account!" Magnetin drew his sword and prepared for combat.

The battle began with Rex using his power to lift up three boulders and throw them at Magnetin, he quickly dodged them and the two went into a struggle match as sword and greataxe met. Rex wasn't joking about his size and strength as he slowly began to push Magnetin back. Seeing Magnetin couldn't hold on much longer, he unleashed a powerful fire breath which caused Rex to break away from the struggle, the flames did scorch him a bit, though. Magnetin quickly ran around the flames and tried to perform an attack from behind, but Rex saw it coming and quickly avoided it. Magnetin that unleashed another fire breath onto the ground in front of him, it missed Rex, but Rex wasn't what he was aiming at. Rex did a gravity-defying jump into the air, only to see that the ground under him is now melting and just touching it with his feet will burn him.

"Nicely done!" Rex said as he landed in a small patch of dirt that hasn't been incinerated yet, but he can't move. Magnetin continued his assault on the Guardian of Earth, who stood his guard. Magnetin seemed to be much faster and powerful when exposed to flames. The smoke made it hard for Rex to even tell which direction Magnetin will come out from. He quickly looked behind himself and saw a pair of eyes when Magnetin emerge from the other end and when in for the kill. It was close as Rex's ax was about to decapitate the young trainee.

Magnetin used his Dragon Cleave on Rex, slashing him once, nothing happened, then Rex began to burn up and fell to the ground, smoldering. A loud boom was heard and a quake was felt as his large body hit the ground. Our hero fell on his rump, panting as he regained his composure. His friends cheered for his victory. Still burned, Rex stood on his feet as he looked at Magnetin.

"Rise up, Magnetin Darkwind, for you are victorious!" Rex said. Magnetin's friends cheered on his well deserved victory.

"Something tells me Rex was holding back…" Andrew, while happy Magnetin won, felt a bit dubious.

Rex took the stone heart off the pedestal. "And now… Your prize… Take this, crush and grind it in your hands and you'll receive the earth element. You'll also receive a pair of boots for a special armor that becomes as strong as you do."

Magnetin took the heart, crushed and grind it with his hands. But by doing this, Rex began to feel his own life force slowly being to grind away as his body slowly turns into soil. "Rex!"

"Why's he turning into soil!?" Andrea exclaimed as none of them knew what was going on.

"Don't stop! In order for you to gain power, we guardians must give up our lives in the process. And don't worry," he then eyes Andrea, "there will be another to take my place."

I… what? Andrea thought to herself when he said that while eying her.

"I have no regrets, I already informed my family of this. Just promise me this… That you'll become a full-fledged Dragon Knight."

"I promise." Magnetin continued as Rex's body slowly turned into soil.

That's my grandson… You've made some great friends… Rex thought to himself. "Death is only the beginning…" And with these last words, Rex's body turned into dust and soil. The soil materialized around Magnetin's feet as he gained his new boots. Silence filled the area as the Draconian spectators let out a roar of mourning. Kamori climbed onto Magnetin's shoulder.

"How you holdin', whelp?" Kamori asked.

"A bit saddened…"

"Well, here's a heads up: this journey won't be a happy-go-lucky one."

"Right…"

"How are you feeling now? Any stronger?"

"I feel no different…"

"Well, I do. Try activating it. The element that you're currently using will also reflect the color of your boots."

Magnetin looked at his boots and watched them change to beige. He then raised an arm and a leg up and made a powerful stomp. This caused a shock wave in front of him and caused the earth to spike up. He did various tricks with the turned up earth. Afterward, he changed the color of the boots back to gray. While the others were impressed, Andrea, of all people, wasn't even paying attention as she was seen stewing in thought of what Rex meant when he looked at her.

Once he was done messing around, Magnetin turned back to the group. "We should get going." Everyone, except for Andrea, which drew notice from her brother.

"Andrea," the alchemist called out to his sister, "we're going."

"Yeah…" Andrea muttered as she got up. She looked back to where Rex stood, seeing the greataxe being stuck in the ground, before following the others outside the dungeon. Time has passed since the group was in the dungeon as it was evening.

As the group re-entered Stone Crow Town, there was a particular scientist at the village, who just left for Oceanus City. As he was leaving, the group caught a small glimpse of the old man as they walked by, except for Andrea (who was still stewing in her thoughts), who also looked back at them.

So that's him, eh? We'll meet properly later.

"Who's that?" Andrew asked as the scientist left their sight. "What's an old timer like him doing in a desert like this? And how did he get here?"

"That man has a history," Kamori said, "but that'll have to be another time. Let's find a place to stay, it's too cold for a whelp to travel through a desert at night."

The group found an inn to spend the night at as well as to chart their next course. "The next guardian is located south of here," Magnetin said as he pointed on the map.

"That's where the ruins of the old elven kingdom are," Anita stated. "What the hell will we be able to find in that wasteland?"

"Your guess is as good as mine," the dragon trainee shrugged.

"Hey, what's wrong with Andrea?" Delphine asked as she took notice of the blacksmith twin, who was not her bombastic, yet straight-forward self and had been silent the entire time they left the dungeon.

"What's wrong, sis?" Andrew asked with concern. "Is it the drinks?"

"Andrew…" Andrea muttered to him. "I think we should head back home for now… I'm not feeling so good…"

Andrew, seeing his sister in distress, noticed that she wasn't sick but something else was going on with her before he turned to the others. "Sorry, Mag, but Andrea and I are going to have to take our leave from this quest of yours…"

"I hope it's nothing too serious," Magnetin said with concern.

"I don't know…" Andrew said with a shrug. "When you return to Oceanus City, come see us, alright?"

With that, the Cashonit Twins went to their room for the night.

"What's wrong with Andrea?" Anita asked with concern.

"I don't know," Delphine said with equal concern. And with that, the group turned in for the night, wondering what tomorrow will bring.

EPISODE 4

Guardian of Light

The main group was up early because the next location was a ways off so they loaded the truck and were about to set off. A caravan was on the way back to Oceanus City to get some supplies, the Cashonit Twins, at Andrea's request, decided to return to Oceanus City as well.

Continuing on with Magnetin's quest, the group drove through the Searing Desert, following the road for a few hours until they got to a site of the ancient ruins of Rummi, an elven civilization. In the distance of these ruins, there was an enormous staircase that looked like it stretched onto the heavens, or at least, it would have had it not crumbled away. The group climbed out of the truck and walked up to the stairs. Delphine actually recognizes this place and was able to read the writing.

"What? Did we get a bogus location?" Anita pout.

"No, this is the location," Magnetin said.

"Not exactly," Delphine explains as she walks up to a glyph and about to place her hand on it. "It's in Sylvan… the language of fairies." Suddenly they got surrounded by a horde of monsters, tigers, bulls, and wolves. There were just too many to count.

"Why are we being attacked all of the sudden?" Anita complained at the sudden attack. "And why all of these beasts!?"

"Only one person I know who's capable of commanding all these beasts at once…" Magnetin said as he prepared for combat. "Francis…"

"Oh, that mutt…" Anita groaned through gritted teeth. She took out Jesse and shot the three coming at her from her left, before taking out the ones that snuck up on her, without even looking.

"Well, they want to party so bad." Magnetin turned to the two as a monster came up from behind as the young trainee's sword punctured its skull. Magnetin turned his head to the monster with a grin. "I've been looking for some targets to fight. Let's not leave them hanging." He grasps the handle with both hands as he spun around, using the monster's body to take out all reckless enough to get too close. Anita grabbed one by the torso and began to whack it with her revolver twice as she fired shots and two monsters. The third whack, she sends it flying into the stairway, taking out another monster that was getting into position.

Magnetin jumped onto a bull monster's back and acted like it was a rodeo, using his free hand to wave his sword around and slice up the unsuspecting when they got closer. He then sets his sword on fire and jammed his sword through the monster's throat, causing it to burn up from within. Magnetin then did a forward flip off the flaming beast and slammed it onto two more monsters before pulling back, causing the impaled monster to fly off and impale another monster that was close to flanking him.

Anita fired a couple of shots that bounced off some of the stone pillars and one shot at Magnetin. Magnetin bends down at the last second as the shot flew over him and hit a monster lunging from his right. The next shots that bounced off the pillars shot some more monsters that were trying to hide. It was saved to say that they were having fun, except for Delphine, who was still focused on the writing. A beast was about to flank her from behind when Delphine just put her arm up, grabbed it, brought it and threw it to Anita, who did a roundhouse to its jaw, the impacted triggered a mechanism in her boot which caused a blade that's stored in the heel reacted and puncture it more to ensure its death.

"Hey, Delphine, you're missing out," Anita stated, but Delphine wasn't even paying attention to the carnage. Magnetin used his new earth powers to rapidly tap the ground with his foot and caused earth spikes to rise up and puncture each monster surrounding him. He just casually yawned and folded his arms.

"There's something here…" Delphine said as she proceeded to place her hand on the glyph. This caused a tremendous amount of light to shine forth, enough to blind the monsters and caused some of them to flee.

This was a familiar feeling to her as a portal opened up from underneath them and pulled them in before closing itself. The light then vanished, allowing the monsters to see again and becoming clueless as to what happened. In the distance, Francis was watching from afar on a beast he had tamed, irate to see that Magnetin escaped him.

"Damn that lizard!" He cursed.

The group then reappeared in the same location, but there is something else. There was no sense of darkness in the area. Everything was nice and pleasant.

"Awwww… We were just getting started," Magnetin sighed in disappointment.

"Great way to spoil our fun, Del," Anita pouted. Delphine was still really out of it.

"This place. We're in Heaven," Delphine spoke.

"Wow, so this is heaven," Anita awed.

"Wait! How do you know of this place, Delphine?" Magnetin asked her.

"I… don't know, I just do." She replied, lost for words. Flying overhead was actually various angels and they saw a female humanoid walk towards them.

It was a female draconian. She had long blonde hair, white eyes, tan skin and a slim build with an average bust. She wore edo period clothing. This was Santa Lightseer, and strapped to her hip was a special katana. She stood at six foot six.

"It appears you've made it, Rex got careless," she said.

"Rex? Then you must be…" Magnetin said.

"A Guardian, yes. I'm called Santa Lightseer, Guardian of Light." She had a stoic, forward personality, but at the same time had a heavenly smile.

"Good Ol' Del has done it again!" Anita grinned.

"Follow me." The group started walking with Santa.

"So do all of you know about me?"

"We have all known about you even before you became a trainee," Santa replied, "so there's no need for secrecy." She then before looking over to Delphine. "And it seems you have a fairy companion as well." This caused Delphine to stop in her tracks.

"Excuse me, what!? Me? A fairy?" Delphine was as shocked as she could be.

"You are able to read Sylvan. All will be explained later." Santa led them to a place similar to Rex's. "I suggest that Rex challenged you with his labyrinth?"

"Do I have to go through another maze or something different?" Magnetin asked.

"Each of us has a different challenge for you," Santa explained. "Mines is an obstacle course you'll have to make through and reach the artifact I set before time's up and without falling. It's a long one, but you just need to reach the artifact. Since we're in Heaven, there are no monsters, but mine will have more things to deal with than Rex's did to make up for it. The time limit is still 15 minutes like Rex's, but no one can help you, alright?"

What does this... have to do with being a Dragon Knight exactly? Anita thought to herself.

"Very well, then. I'm ready."

"It'll be best if your companion stays with me as well." Santa pointed at Kamori. He flew off Magnetin's shoulder and onto Santa's. "Jump onto the spring. It'll project you up to the platform."

Anita took out her stopwatch. "I'll keep track of the time." She set it to 15 minutes. Magnetin jumped onto the spring and got shot upward and landed on the platform held up by a pillar. There was a staircase that went around the pillar and the top of it. There was a bridge that led over to a number of moving platforms up to a tunnel that was rolling counter-clockwise and near the end of it had a few gaps in it. At the halfway marker, there was a group of rotating platforms with rolling spikes rotating in the opposing direction of the platforms themselves. There were two of these, with one of the rolling spikes being higher than the others. And the last part was another tunnel that was rotating clockwise and had more gaps. He couldn't see much of it, though, because he was behind the pillar.

"Whelps, don't try this stuff at home!" Kamori grinned with an aside glance.

"Who are you talking to?" Anita muttered.

"Ready?"

"Let's get serious!" Magnetin grinned as he grabbed the railings.

"GO!" He started to run up the staircase and crossed a bridge over to several moving platforms. Using position jumps to reach each platform while trying not to fall off. Some platforms were moving in weird directions and all over the place, Magnetin had to dodge a few coming his way, and some had blades on them. After crossing it, he continued through a rolling tunnel. It was hard to keep one's footing in there as the tunnel was rolling constantly, and sometimes roll the other way, but the boots kept Magnetin balanced. He was halfway to the artifact, but now he had to jump on platforms with the rolling spikes. Magnetin jumped onto one and jumped as each spike passed until he made it to the other platform with the high spikes so he had to duck down. He was very close to the artifact and made it to the rotating tunnel. Magnetin quickly jumped in as the opening came his way and decided to wait, but soon realized that the tunnel was going the other way. Seeing that, he ran down to the center of the tunnel and waited to see if the tunnel would make a complete turn. It did but started to turn the other way again, this was Magnetin's chance as he quickly ran down the tunnel and quickly jumped onto the platform and grabbed the artifact, which appeared to be a grail. This made a platform appear before him to take him back to the arena. Magnetin presented the grail to Santa.

"Very good indeed. You've completed it in 8 minutes flat."

"It's simple once you get into the right groove." Magnetin grinned.

"Now follow me back to the arena."

"Question… When Rex gave me his power…"

"He sacrificed himself, yes. But he's not exactly dead," Santa explained. "You see, whenever a draconian dies, our entire beings return to the very element itself or we can pass it on by merging with another should the situation present itself." This brought relief to Magnetin, now knowing they are not giving up their lives in vain. Kamori hopped onto his back.

"Santa will be harder than Rex was and she's a lot faster than you are. Your advantage is that she is honorable and doesn't use underhanded tactics or such other things that can dishonor her."

"Should I fight her honorably?"

"That's up to you. And you also have the earth at your side as well."

The two walked into the arena before Delphine intervened. "Um… Aren't you going to tell me about me being a fairy? I've been living as a human all my life and now I've learned that I am a fairy."

"If you have the patients, please wait until this is over, the angels here will tell you afterward. After all, you are a patient woman, are you not?"

"But this is just so new and confusing to me."

"You'll get your chance to set the record straight, Blue Girl," Kamori informed.

"Unlike Rex, I've been prepared for you. And I can face you with my full strength." Santa places the grail onto the pedestal. She moved into position, placing her hand on the handle as they were ready to fight. Santa didn't seem to do anything, except for a beam of light that shot forth. While they look like beams of light, they're actually swords made of light. Magnetin quickly dodged it as it pierces through a structure that was a few yards behind him. More beams of light shot forth as Magnetin continued to dodge, getting hit by one could mean certain doom. Magnetin looked at Santa for a moment and noticed that she hadn't moved at all from her stance, but saw that the earth around her feet was dug down slightly. She was moving, but at a speed the naked eye can't register. Magnetin activated the earth element and decided to go on the offense. As his foot tapped the ground, a shock wave shook the arena, but that didn't keep Santa off balance. Magnetin while kneeling rapidly tapped the ground with his heel, causing dozens of earth spikes to rise up on all sides, and now Santa, who quickly dodge as they rammed into each other. Magnetin pulled up 5 boulders from the ground and threw them one at a time at her. She evades the first one but then saw the other four ganging up on her and the other boulder had turned around and surrounded her in the air.

"Impressive." While being a few seconds away from being crushed, Santa quickly grabbed her katana and performed a widespread light spin attack to shred through the boulders. Beams of light cut through the boulders like a hot knife through butter. Magnetin then charged in and the two went into a sword clash as dirt, fire and light raged throughout all directions. The two combatants broke away and decided to finish it with a standoff. As the last boulder, that was still in the air, hit the ground, the two jumped into the air and quickly rushed forward with a single slice. The two stood motionless as blood spilled onto the arena, both sides were bleeding, now it was a matter of endurance. Santa's body slowly fell onto the floor. Magnetin, despite having a sword slice through his chest, had won. After a few moments, Santa raised to her feet and turned to Magnetin.

"You've victorious, Magnetin." Santa congratulated him. She walked over to the grail and presented it to him.

"When you drink from this, you'll gain the light element and the gauntlets to your armor," Santa explained. "And thus will end my existence. Now drink up." Magnetin proceeds to drink the contents of the grail. A pair of gauntlets began materializing on his hands. Santa's body began to fade away into the light. Delphine quickly approached her.

"You can't just leave me like this!" She wanted to know about herself.

"Right… Take my sword, dear and all will be explained to you." Santa held her katana out for Delphine to grab. Once she grabbed the sheath, Santa was able to speak to her telepathically. ***All will be explained to you, my successor…***

"What?" Delphine gasped.

"Death is only the beginning…" She smiled as she vanished from sight.

The two armor pieces changed to yellow. He activated the earth element to kick the last boulder in the air and turned back to the light element and shot beams of light at the Boulder, they easily pierced through the boulder, and he didn't even move a muscle. And each sword slash shoots a beam and slices the boulder in half.

While Magnetin was testing his new stuff out, Santa had merged with Delphine as she held the katana in her hands as an angel appeared before her. The angel appeared to be wearing majestic armor along with a hood. The oddest thing Delphine had thought about this angel was him lacking a face, only a shroud of darkness was seen in the hood.

"I'm a fairy."

"Indeed, you are a fairy that had died once before being reincarnated one as well." The angel replied to her. "You see when a fairy dies, they can either resurrect themselves within a large radius of where they died or back at any fairy fountain, or be reincarnated into a new body, which you did the latter. However, fairies are unfit to take care of a newborn, so your great fairy mother took and delivered you to that sinful family. We questioned that decision at first, but you rose above and now you have friends." The angel looked at the katana as he kneels before her, as a big group of angels surrounded Delphine, kneeling as well. "Please take the Kyuseishu, merge with Santa and transcend."

As Delphine grabbed the handle of the katana, the angels began to recite a chant in Latin. Delphine closed her eyes and felt a tremendous amount of light surround and filled her, becoming the light itself. She felt warmth, grace, and love. She was given a large circular shield, new full plate armor, and her own sword, it looked like a longsword, with the handle designed like a cross. The armor matched her hair color and the trimmings matched her eye color. Delphine's eyes opened up as all the knowledge had filled her mind, mostly about herself, her sisters and her great fairy mother.

"I remember…" Delphine spoke as she looked at her new set of gear. "I am the Fairy of Abjuration. I have six sisters and a great fairy mother."

"Congratulations. Santa has merged with you, allowing you to transcend into a Dragon Paladin and became a Fairy Dragonborn. And that sword you have was called the Kyuseishu when Santa weld it, but you can call it Savior, and your shield is called Valkyrie. And it has the power to revive anyone from the brink of death. It can also be used to send the dearly departed to the afterlife, where they may rest in peace. In a few days, you'll start to grow wings." Delphine just stood silent.

"We should get going and head back to Oceanus City," Kamori informed.

"I advise seeking the Guardians of Wind and Water. They can probably make traveling easier for you. Good luck to you all. Even though you can't see us, we're always watching." The group was teleported out of heaven and reappeared in the real world again. All the monsters were gone, though. Delphine strapped her longsword on her waist and strapped her shield on her left arm. Anita took out her truck capsule and they drove off.

"How'd y'all think Andrea's holding up?" Anita asked. "She seemed to be pretty distressed when they left."

"I don't know," Delphine said, before thinking to herself. ***But what I do know is that I know how she feels…***

In the distance, a humanoid was watching the trio as they returned to Oceanus City.

It was a male draconian. He had the head of a dragon, orange eyes, cyan skin, a hulking build, a stubby tail and a pair of dragon wings. He wore light blue chainmail armor. This was Draco Asunder, and in his hand, he held a greataxe. He stood at a whopping seven foot six. "You're becoming stronger. But time is running short."

Meanwhile…

As the Cashonit Twins were taking the caravan back to Oceanus City. Andrea was just sitting in the back in a fetal position, contemplating on everything that happened. Andrew was talking with one of the caravan members.

"We should be reaching the city shortly," The caravan member said to Andrew.

"I thank you for this," Andrew said with a smile. "I'll return the favor by setting up a supply line at the Cashonit Stop."

"Oh, no, the materials you had provided for us was more than enough," another caravan member said. "But if you want, we wouldn't mind trading with you in the future."

Andrew continued to talk while Andrea continued to stew in her thoughts of what Rex said to her. *He looked at me when he said another will take his place... Does he mean... me?*

Along the High Seas Saga

EPISODE 5

Sailing through Dark Waters

After a long drive back to Oceanus City, the trio headed to Anita's workshop so she can finish up her latest invention: A jetpack and a pair of jet boosters.

"I'll need to work out some bugs. If the next place is located in the ocean, then we'll need something special," she started to work on her invention.

"While you're working on that, we should see if there are any boats available," Delphine suggested.

"I want to see how Andrew and Andrea are doing first, especially Andrea," Magnetin added. "So why don't we split up then. We can get more done that way." Magnetin and Delphine left Anita's workshop and went their separate ways, Delphine headed to the docks while Magnetin walked down the street to the Cashonit Shop.

Along the way, Magnetin saw Cinghiale, the same orc from the other day. He was leaning against the wall, pounding the side in agony.

"I'm such a fool!" Cinghiale cursed.

"Hey, what's wrong?" Magnetin asked. The orc recognized the voice and quickly turned around only to scream.

"Not you again! I-I-I'm not…" Cinghiale tried to back up against the wall, trembling in fear. Despite the size difference, the orc was scared shitless of Magnetin.

"Oh, calm down. It looks like you're sober now. So, can you tell me what's wrong?"

"It was the other day when I bump into you guys, as soon as I got home that night, my fiance left me!"

"Oh! Sorry to hear about that… How did that happen?"

"One of her friends saw what happened between us and told her what happened. My buddies and I were celebrating my marriage and, you know the rest. She couldn't live with someone who did what I did and she had a problem with my drinking. But I'm not a heavy drinker, I swear! I just had one too many!" Magnetin was speechless of the orc's fiance as he felt responsible to some degree.

"Hey, look, I am terribly sorry. But what happened is between you and your fiance."

"What…can I do?"

"Find your fiance and try to make it up to her."

"I'll try! T-thank you. And I'm sorry about bumping into your friend and calling you a lizard."

"Hey, I had bad experiences with being called a lizard before. But you aren't a bad orc, so no worries. I better get going, see ya around." Magnetin waves Cinghiale goodbye as he continued to the Cashonit Shop. When he got there, he only saw Andrew tending the shop.

"Hey, Andrew, we're back! How were things on your trip back?"

"Things went pretty peaceful for the most part," Andrew replied with a smile. "Managed to snag a deal with some caravans and opened up a supply chain. The caravans provide us materials, we buy the materials, we make stuff with them, and then we sell them. Business will be booming… once Andrea gets out of her slump, that is."

"How is your sister by the way?"

"I don't know, she hasn't talked to me about what happened at the cave with Rex," Andrew said with concern before turning to the back room that led to their bedrooms. "Normally, she'd be hammering away at her forge, making the next batch of weapons and armor while I brew the next batch of potions. Now, she won't even show that bombastic personality of hers."

"Hey, your sister is one tough human, she'll bounce back eventually," Magnetin said. "'The weak become strong, the strong become stronger.' As the draconian saying goes." He then looked around. "I don't see your father either. Usually, he'd be manning the store."

"We really don't know. He wasn't here when we got back. The attendants said he went out shortly after we've left and hasn't returned since. I wonder what happened…" Andrew replied, also showing concern. "I know father wasn't thrilled with us leaving, but still. In any case, we've been thinking of expanding our shop to all other cities across the world. Probably use some sort of teleportation spell at various points to bring them here."

"Well," Magnetin spoke up, "the next guardians are located across the sea so we'll need a ship to travel across it. Delphine's trying to get us a one so we can travel across the ocean and Anita's working on some new inventions."

"I'm surprised she hasn't got around to mass market her stuff yet," Andrew said, but bits in his voice betraying the eagerness wanting to sell some of Anita's inventions and make a profit from them.

"You know Anita cares about quality over quantity. Plus, most of her stuff is still in beta testing. Though, those capsule things are very effective."

"Well, we wouldn't be interested if it weren't good," Andrew stated. "'If it's not good, it's not worth selling!'"

Before the conversation would continue, they suddenly heard the sounds of people screaming as they ran by. Some were screaming: "MONSTERS! IN THE CITY PLAZA! RUN!" Some of them actually came into the shop for shelter.

"What's going on out here!?" Andrew exclaimed, wanting answers as to why random people are barging into the shop.

"Monsters! They're attacking the city!" One of the people exclaimed.

"How did monsters get into the city!?"

"We don't know!" Another of the people exclaimed. "Somebody do something!"

"I'll go," Magnetin said as he stood tall.

"Wait, before you go, take this!" Andrew handed Magnetin a super potion. "This is a lot stronger than what you have right now. Use it as a last resort."

"Thanks!"

"Go rip them a new one for us!" Andrew said patting his friend on the back. Magnetin hurried outside and charged with battle.

While all this was happening, Andrea was sitting on her bed in the same fetal position as before when she heard people screaming outside. This was enough for her to take notice.

Meanwhile, as Magnetin was doing his thing, Delphine was on her way to the docks as she came across a female humanoid weeping.

This was a female orc. She had long black hair, black eyes, green skin and a muscular build with a large bust. She wore commoner clothing. This was Soraka. She stood at six foot nine.

"Madam? What's wrong?" Delphine asked.

"Oh, what have I done!? I shut out my one chance of happiness!" Soraka cried.

"Excuse me!" Delphine got the crying orc to turn around.

"Oh, I'm sorry, dear."

"Can you tell me what happened?"

"One of my girlfriends told me that my fiancee was drinking heavily and almost got himself into a fight. I got so mad, I broke up with him!" Soraka wailed. Delphine covered her ears as it was painful. "And now…"

"Wait…" Delphine thought back to the other day when that male orc almost wailed on her. This widens her eyes. "I actually ran into him the other day, literally. He was all smashed."

"Were you the one!? Oh, I'm terribly sorry for his actions!" Soraka needed to blow her nose. Delphine handed her handkerchief over to the crying orc, who immediately used it. It was completely covered in snot as Delphine, with a look of disgust, puts it in the disposal bin nearby.

"That's what happens when someone is smashed, they have no control over their own actions. I'm sure he's not always like that, madam," Delphine tried to calm the female orc down.

"You're right. He's a hard worker and real sweet."

"I'm sure he feels just as terrible about this as you do."

"What can I do!?"

"Find him and makeup with him. Believe me, no one deserves to go through all their lives and not be happy."

"You're absolutely right!" Soraka, despite being shorter than Delphine, gave her a bear hug, nearly crushing the fairy's spine, before she ran off. Delphine felt her lower back ache as she rubbed it a bit. Regaining her composure, she proceeds to the docks. She approaches the captain and tells them her situation.

"You see, captain. We need to use one of your boats so we can find the Guardians of Wind and Water. And this is the only place where we can rent a boat."

"I see your problem. Unfortunately, we can't do that. There's a storm raging out there and it's blocking our route to the other continents so all our shipments are delayed."

Delphine then pondered that there was a storm stirred up the same moment Magnetin needed a ship. "This is probably the next trial then. We have to travel into the eye of the storm."

"Listen here, lass. This may be important to you, but most, if not all, of my crewmen, have families to support."

"Then we'll take a boat and sail it ourselves."

"Hogwash! What can landlubbers like you know the first thing about sailing without a crew? And into a raging storm, no less?"

"We can't just wait until the storm dies out?"

"Storms can't last forever, lass."

"But what if this one does?"

"Captain!" One of the crewmen shouted from outside.

"What is it, skipper!?"

"Sea monsters!!! They're coming up from the shores! And headed this way!" Yards away from the direction he was running from, Delphine saw an army of sea monsters, that seek to rule the ocean, jumping out of the ocean and swarming the docks, she jumped down the balcony that she was on and ran towards the sea monsters.

"Lass, what are you doing!? ARE YOU INSANE!? YOU'LL BE KILLED!! GET BACK HERE!!!" The captain yelled in an attempt to get Delphine to stop her charge, but she ignored him. Armed with her sword and shield, she stood her ground as the sea monsters grew closer. This was the perfect opportunity to test her swordplay.

With Anita, she was fine-tuning her jetpack and jet boosters and began to test it out. She attached the jet boosters to her boots and strapped the jet pack onto her back. It started to hum as Anita's began to slowly move a few inches off the floor.

"YES!" She was excited that it worked better than she expected. She took this time to walk out of her workshop, grabbing her pack of her special gum and test it for herself. She was having the time of her life. "YEEEEEEEE-HAAAAAAAAW!!!" She performed various of tricks. How jet packs work is that it takes in the hydrogen stored in the air and sends them through the filters and charges the jetpack. The jet boosters provide extra speed to the feet and allow her kicks to be more powerful due to the sheer impact. Her excitement, however, was short-lived as she saw a flock of birds coming at her, carrion and birds of prey. "Okay... I don't know what's going on, but it looks like they wanna fight..." She grinned with even more excitement as she branded her revolver as a light engulfed her free hand, materializing into a semi-automatic pistol that had a golden finish and a silver handle with the name "James" engraved on its barrel. She didn't know how she got the pistol, but she felt like a whole new arsenal was available to her. "Jesse! James! Let's rock, boys!"

Back at the Cashonit Shop, Andrea finally got on her feet and stumbled her way to the main entrance and saw all of the people hiding in the shop. She then looked and gasped as she saw Andrew fighting a gorilla that had managed to barge into the shop, and he wasn't doing well.

"This sucks..." Andrew groaned in pain he received from fighting the gorilla. He tried to pull out a potion to heal himself, but the gorilla whacked the potion out of his hand and pounced on him.

"Andrew!" Andrea exclaimed as she grabbed her warhammer and struck the gorilla on the skull with all her might. This was enough to kill the gorilla in one single hit. "Get your hands off him, you damn, dirty ape!"

"Andrea…" Andrew groaned before he passed out from his injuries as his sister grabbed the potion he dropped.

With Magnetin, he ran down the road and made it to the plaza, he saw bodies lying on the ground, covered in blood. The monsters were killing innocent people. The police tried their best to fend them off, but the monsters have proven to be too strong for them. The police weren't letting up.

"Hold the line, men!" The lead officer commanded. He was determined to stop the monsters with the look on his face.

"Have your men stand down, officer," Magnetin said as he approached and drew his sword.

"Look here, sonny, it's dangerous. We have our finest men here and even they can't take these monsters down."

"I don't want to argue here, but these monsters aren't those everyday ones. They've already killed some of your men, however, I can fight them!" Magnetin explained.

"Go! We'll cover your back!" Magnetin hurried and charged at the oncoming monsters and took two down with a single slice each. Magnetin beckoned them to attack him instead. It worked as the monsters drew their attention to him. Kamori, who flew off Magnetin's shoulder, sits on top of a building and looks at the random destruction the monsters have created. He sees Magnetin, Delphine, and Anita all fighting their own horde of monsters.

"Francis… You just can't let it go… Can you?" Kamori sighs. "Well, guys, let's see how far your new powers take you." On another building, Francis was observing the mayhem his monsters were causing. Something was off about him, though.

"Let's see how well you do without your friends to back you up now, lizard!" Francis laughed before looking over to the docks. "Wait, sea monsters?"

It started with Delphine as she proceeded to decapitate several of the sea monsters by throwing her shield like a boomerang. A few tried to jump her, but she effortlessly dodged around them like she was a ballerina, despite wearing full plate armor, swinging her blade around like a baton. After wiping a few clean, Delphine threw her blade into the air and laid down on her back.

One of the sea monsters tried to attack her while she was prone, and she slightly moved her body left and right to avoid. Her blade came down and decapitated the monster as she quickly grabbed its handle with her teeth and performed a backward flip into the air and performed twirls that were, again, impossible for someone in full plate to do gracefully, while catching her shield.

"The way she's fighting… It's almost like dancing," one of the sailors commented, captivated by Delphine's grace.

"But she's in full plate armor, though…" Another sailor said.

"This armor is way lighter than it looks," Delphine said with a shrug. "Almost like I'm wearing nothing at all."

Back with Anita, she was having a blast, literally, as she was blowing up a group of monsters by throwing grenades at them and shooting some grenades to cause a chain reaction of explosions. A bunch of monsters tried to swarm her and she reacted by using one of her jet boosters to quickly spin her around for a powerful roundhouse as she shot them all with her handguns. One was still alive, which she wrapped her legs around its head and shot three of them approaching her from behind. She then grabbed a stick of her special gum and began to chew it as she continued to shoot them all.

Back with Magnetin, he petrified a large group with the stone breath and watched them turn to dust. Then he used the light power and destroyed another large group with the sword beams of light, from his fingers and decapitated and dismembered them. With the elements of earth and light have made Magnetin much more powerful, he was mowing down the monsters like there was no tomorrow. The policemen were impressed after seeing Magnetin's power.

"Man, that's a powerful warrior we have there," one officer commented.

"Aye, he's a strong lad," another commented. Magnetin used his tail and grabbed one of the monsters by the neck and flung it around and used it to strike all monsters that got close. Another monster manages to conceal itself and tries to flank Magnetin.

"Shit!" One of the officers cursed as they tried to shoot the monster, but someone came up to the monster and punched it in the face. Magnetin looked up to see that it was the orc from earlier.

"I owe you one!"

"No need. Because we're even," He turned to a group of monsters and shouted: "Any and all of you that lays a finger on him will be better off dead!" With no weapons or armor, the orc fought them with just his fists.

Francis growled as he saw his monsters getting wiped from them. Even though he can control monsters, they only hold a little bit of his power. He can control armies of monsters, but they'll be no stronger.

"How about if I control just one big monster?" Francis began to plan. "Yes. And I know just the monster." He releases his grip on the monsters. This caused all of them to stop their attacks and look around, confused.

With Magnetin.

"What's going on?" Cinghiale asked.

"Seems like they were being controlled, and I know who," Magnetin said as a matter of fact.

"Okay, what's going on here?" Anita demanded to know, disappointed that she didn't get a chance to perform a special move. After a few minutes, the monsters went back to from where they came from. "Awwwwwwww…" Anita was disappointed. "That's complete bull…" She then descends herself back to the plaza, where the orc, and the policemen were all stumped.

"I knew that monsters don't attack cities on their own, they only attack those who come near their habitat or become hostile due to some disturbance, like that earthquake a few days ago." Magnetin said as he knew who did this. "Francis…"

"That mutt's taking this just a little too far!" Anita growled.

"But commanding a horde of monsters to terrorize a city isn't his style…" Just then, they heard static on the officer's radio.

"Come in! We got trouble on the dock!" It was the captain. "There're sea monsters swarming the docks and they unleashed some kind of monster attacking our ships!"

"Sea monsters? Here!?" Magnetin muttered.

The transmission continued. "We have important cargo! If we lose the ships, we can't transport the cargo to the other two continents! And there is this blue lass here that is taking on this monster alone!"

"Blue lass!?" Magnetin and Anita said in unison before looking at each other. "Delphine!" The two hurried down the road to the docks as fast as they could. The orc followed them.

"Why are you coming along!?"

"I haven't repaid my debt, yet! Plus, I'm the first mate!" This shocked both Magnetin and Anita. At the docks, Delphine was having a bit of trouble fighting the monster as it didn't have a physical form. It was just a blob of some kind of gooey liquid and it was covering most of the ship with its goo. It had a nucleus core inside the gooey liquid, but its shell prevented most attacks from striking it.

"GET AWAY FROM THAT, LASS! IT WILL EAT YOU ALIVE!" The captain yelled at the top of his lungs and warned her with all his might, but she wouldn't stop.

"I have to at least try something!" Delphine was determined to defeat the blob monster, as she saw its nucleus moving. Delphine quickly dodged the blob's attacks and made her way to the nucleus, she tried piercing through the goo, but the nucleus quickly moved through its body freely. Delphine's sword was now stuck in the goo and couldn't pull it out. "No!" The goo of the monster quickly blocked her escape and trapped her in a gooey bubble. Luckily for her, her head wasn't trapped, but she couldn't move her body due to the density before she felt her back itching like mad, and couldn't reach for it. "My back!"

Magnetin and Cinghiale just made it to the docks. Anita went back to her shop to get something.

"CAPTAIN!!!" The orc yelled. This drew the captain's attention.

"Cinghiale!" The captain responded.

"Where's the monster!?"

"You're not fighting it! It's already eating ship 101 and that blue lass is--"

"Delphine! I'm coming!" Magnetin charged towards the ship.

"Hold on there, lad!" The captain warned, but no avail. "What's with these landlubbers…?"

Magnetin ran down the pathway to the ship and just saw Delphine get trapped in a bubble. "Delphine!"

"Magnetin! Don't come any closer. Or you'll get trapped as well!"

"I'm not leaving you there!" Magnetin jumped onto the ship, switching to the light element and tried to shoot beams to pierce through the liquid ooze, but the beams got pushed back, deflected and changed their course by the density. One got through and was almost close enough to strike the nucleus, but it evaded and pierced through the captain's quarters of the ship.

"And whatever you do, please don't damage me ship in the process!" The captain cried as the beam pierced through the ship's walls.

"Let me help!" Cinghiale called out.

"Stay over there!" Magnetin called back. "The weak point's the nucleus, but it's moving too fast... Even faster than the speed of light!"

"Magnetin! Your feet!" Delphine called out. The blob monster's liquid body had caught Magnetin's feet and already worked its way up his legs. The density made it impossible for Magnetin to move his feet.

"Shit!" Magnetin cursed his luck. This blob monster was stronger and smarter than it looked. The blob then pulls Magnetin over to Delphine and traps both of them in one bubble filled with slime each. Their heads were out of the bubble, though.

"NO!"

Magnetin went changed earth element and used all of his strength to burst out of the liquid while Delphine was doing the same, but was also dealing with her back. The two felt their skin slowly being ripped off as the blob monster went in for the kill. "You can help any time now, Anita!" Right on cue, Anita appeared flying through the air, she had something on her belt.

"Here I come to save the day!" She grabbed the device from her belt and pointed at the blob's liquid body. It looked like a Taser gun and was set to 1000 volts. "Eat Taser!" The voltage hit the liquid surface and spread throughout its entire body, including the nucleus.

"Don't like it? Well, too bad!" Anita turned up the voltage to 3000. She shot another and hit the liquid surface again, this dealt more damage to its nucleus.

"Quit toying with it and finish it!" Delphine shouted.

"Very well. I've had my fun." Anita turned the voltage all the way up to 500,000 volts. "I only have two shots if I put it this high, better make it count…" She aimed the Taser gun at the liquid body, but it whacked Anita out of the air and the Taser gun out of her hand, onto the deck of the ship near Magnetin's tail. Slowly and carefully, he moved his tail and reached for the Taser gun and wrapped it around the handle and pointed it at their bubble prison. The blob was focused on Anita, whose leg was caught by the blob's liquid arm, she tried to pull herself free, but still, the blob's liquid ooze was too strong. "Okay, this is what I get for being cocky…"

"Brace yourself for voltage, Del!" Magnetin quickly tightens his grip on his tail and zapped their bubble prison, this shocked them both as the bubble prison dissipated. The blob noticed this and tried to whack the Taser gun out of Magnetin's tail into the ocean.

"No! The Taser!" Magnetin sees the Taser gun going over the other side of the ship, he tried running but the ooze grabbed his tail. At that moment, though, Delphine's backstopped itching and finally grew blue bird wings. "Whoa, Delphine! You can fly!" Using this last chance, she quickly spread her wings and flew over the ship and grabbed the gun before it hit the water. She then flew up to liquid ooze on the side of the ship, jammed the Taser in the ooze, tuning the volts to its limit, using her own energy source to recharge it, and pulled the trigger sending 1,000,000 volts of electricity through its liquid body and shocking the three of them as well. The nucleus also felt the voltage so much, it exploded and caused the liquid ooze to slowly dissipate. Some of the oozes remained.

"Captain, did they defeat the monster?"

"Aye, the landlubbers did it." The captain manages to say, amazed at what he saw. The Taser gun itself used up all its power and shutdown. Delphine flew up and made it back to the ship as it started to rain. All three of them were charcoal and their hair frizz.

"My back feels so much better now. I feel lighter." Delphine sighed in relief, sniffing the air. "And I smell ecstasy." Anita takes the Taser gun from Delphine.

"Nice save there, Delphine." Magnetin congratulated her. "And you've both found a way to fly!"

"Looks like it's out of power," Anita sighed at the Taser gun. "Oh well, I'll charge it up later."

"You did it! You slew the beast!" Cinghiale cheered.

"You're that orc…" Delphine gasped.

"Cinghiale is my name. And I'm the first mate here."

"He helped me when I was protecting the plaza," Magnetin replied. "But there's no time to celebrate…" Magnetin said with a stern look. "Francis! Where are you!?" Kamori flew down and landed on the edge of the ship.

"Nice work," Kamori commented. "Unfortunately, Francis is LONG gone. He wasn't disappointed or anything because he now knows the extent of your powers. And he'll most likely command an even stronger monster."

"Cinghiale!" A voice was heard. It was Soraka, the female orc that Delphine helped earlier. She was crying as she ran towards the ship.

"Soraka! My honey bun!" Cinghiale said in response and the two embraced each other. Both Magnetin and Delphine were surprised to find out that they managed to help out two people who happened to be lovers. The female Orc looked over and saw Delphine.

"Oh, it's you, dear. Thank you so much for giving me the courage to find my love again." Soraka said before she turned to her fiance. "I want to say that I'm sorry…"

"You don't have to apologize, my love. I was the one at fault after all."

"No, I am just as much to blame as you. I keep jumping to conclusions and losing my temper." She confessed as well. "The wedding is still on." This caused all the crewmen to cheer that their captain's first mate's wedding is still going on.

"I'm happy for you," the captain approached.

"Captain."

As the crew was talking amongst themselves, Cinghiale looked towards Magnetin, who was talking to Delphine.

"So all this time we helped them both out."

"It would seem so."

"I want to thank you both for saving my marriage," Cinghiale said to the both of them.

"No worries, but we can't rest now," Magnetin said, focusing on the task at hand. "We still need to find a way to get to where the Guardians of Wind and Water are."

"I have tried asking the captain for a ship to sail, no go," Delphine said. "I suspect that this storm IS the next trial and won't let up until we reach them."

"The storm they created must have reached all the way here," Kamori added.

"They're expecting us," Anita summed it up. "And a nice way to start off a greeting session."

"You need a ship?" Cinghiale interjected. "Captain!" He drew the attention of his captain and crewmates. "I want to help them. They save my love and I owe them much. So, please captain, let me sail a ship to their destination."

"You're not sailing this storm along! I'm coming too!" A crew member said.

"For our first mate, Cinghiale!" Another said. Most of the crew was set on helping them out. The captain had no other choice.

"Alright, alright," the captain gave up, "it's gonna take a strong crew to make it through this, though."

"We'll let you decide on that," Magnetin said, before looking at the sky and seeing it getting darker, but not because of the rain clouds, the sun was setting. "We should head back for now. It's getting dark." As the crew set up for the voyage ahead, Magnetin and Delphine went back to her house, while Anita went back to her workshop, but Delphine had a slight problem: her wings. "Uh-oh… I can't put my wings away…" They had a long night with Delphine's wings.

Back at the Cashonit Shop, Andrea had given the potion to Andrew and gave him a chance to recover while tending to the people who ran into their shop. After a while, it was safe outside and the people cleared the shop. This left Andrea the corpse of the gorilla that attacked Andrew to clean up. "I need to speak with the others, hopefully they'll still be in town tomorrow."

At a distance, another humanoid was watching the trio.

It was a female draconian. She had medium-length brown hair, hazel eyes, fair skin, a very long tail, a pair of green dragon wings and a slender build with a large bust. She wore a green and yellow chain shirt over leather armor. This was Lyndis Skyscorcher, and strapped to her waist was a rapier. She stood at six foot six.

Lyndis was applauding them. "Nicely done. You have definitely gotten more powerful. But I'm afraid of what's to come for you." She then turned to eye the Cashonit Twins before she vanished from sight.

EPISODE 6

Eye of the Storm

Morning broke, but it was still raining since yesterday. The clouds blocked the sun, making it look gloomy. The group went back to the docks to see if their ship was ready. Cinghiale was on the ship, tightening the mainsail to the belaying pins and waved that time. The two entered the captain's quarters and walked up to him, who was examining the map of the ocean between the continents, trying to estimate where the eye of the storm is. That's where the Guardians of Wind and Water are located. There were a total of 13 crew members going on this voyage, not including Cinghiale and the captain.

"Any luck?" Magnetin asked.

"Nay, I can't pinpoint the eye of the storm, lad," the captain replied. "It's almost like the eye is moving. Yesterday the eye was here." He points at a spot on the map. "Today, it's now, here." He points at another spot on the other side of an island. Magnetin pointed at the island.

"That's the spot."

"The Tropical Islands. You sure?" Cinghiale asked.

"The way the captain examined from where it was to where it is now; It almost did a 180 degree orbit around the island in the last twelve or so hours. So this is the spot."

"Will we be departing so, lad?"

"Yeah, the sooner we get there the sooner this storm can calm."

"Very well. I'll inform my crew to set sail. We'll be sailing on a ship called the SS Cifelli, she was specially made to withstand rough seas." The captain left.

While this was going on, the Cashonit Twins finished what they were doing and rendezvoused with Delphine. The twins were surprised to see her in full plate armor and with a pair of wings.

"Del!?" Andrew gasped. "Is that you!?"

"Yes, it is," Delphine said with a giggle. "The same Delphine Lightwind who had transcended from acolyte to paladin."

"So you're a paladin now?" Andrea asked. "How did that happen?"

"It was went Magnetin had finished with the Guardian of Light, Santa," Delphine recalled what happened. "Before she gave her life, she handed me her katana and declared me to be her successor. That's how I got all this new gear. The bird wings came later." Delphine displayed her loadout to the twins.

Successor... Her too... Andrea thought as she recalled what Rex said. "How does it feel?"

"I feel swell, actually," Delphine said with a smile. "Especially since I found out I'm a fairy. Well, fairy dragonborn to be exact."

"So you were a fairy all this time?" Andrew asked in an impressed tone. "Find anything else out?"

"I am also the fairy of abjuration, have six sisters and a great fairy mother," Delphine added. "They're somewhere in the world, and I hope to find them once I'm done helping Magnetin on his quest."

"Abjuration?" Andrew asked.

"I believe it's one of the schools of magic," Delphine stated. "Need to look into it more when I get the chance."

"Hey, Del…" Andrea said as she walked up to the paladin. "Be real with me…" She was trying to speak but she didn't want anyone else to hear.

"Oh, of course," Delphine said with a confirming nod before pulling Andrea aside to look at the ocean and extending a wing to keep others from hearing their conversation. "This is about what happened with Rex?"

"Yes," Andrea nodded. "When he said there would be another to take his place as he looked at me. I think he was referring to me taking his place."

"So Rex chose you to be his successor," Delphine said, putting two-and-two together. "As Santa chose me to be her's."

"How were you able to decide on becoming a dragonborn so easily?" Andrea asked.

Delphine thought for a moment before speaking. "Well, I don't doubt that I had loads of questions running through my head. But instead of contemplating on 'what if', I decided despite of what might happen. And here I am."

"And if I decide on it, I will become a dragonborn as well," Andrea said, "right?"

"Hey, I know you're scared," Delphine said with an assuring smile, "I was too. But I know that this is a decision only you can make. No one else can force you."

"What about Andrew?" Andrea asked.

Delphine turned to the brother, saying, "I'm sure we'll figure something out."

"Figure what out?" Andrew asked as he was not privy to this conversation. By then, Anita walked on by.

"What the future will hold," Delphine said to Andrew before turning back to Andrea. "Magnetin, Anita and I will be leaving shortly, so we won't be there for you, but you still have your brother." She then pats the blacksmith on the back. "I'm sure you'll figure it out." And with that, Delphine walked on the walkway leading to the ship.

On the ship, Cinghiale was talking with Magnetin as Delphine joined up with them. "And I'll show you to your rooms." Cinghiale led them under the deck and to two separate rooms. "The ladies' room is to the left. Magnetin, you'll be sleeping in my room just across the corridor, I have an extra bed. Make yourselves comfortable, I must continue with my duties before we set sail." Cinghiale walked back down the corridor, Magnetin and Kamori headed into their room, while Delphine and Anita settled in theirs. There are two separate beds, one for Magnetin and Kamori, while the other is for Cinghiale.

Magnetin sat on the bed as Kamori flew off of his shoulder and landed on the bed.

"What should we do once we're done with the Guardians of Wind and Water?" Magnetin asked his companion. Delphine heard Magnetin talking and turned to him.

"We can go to either continent and search for two of the remaining four Guardians."

"Can you tell me about the Guardians of Wind and Water? By the presence of that plural, I suspect that there's two?"

"They are siblings. Tempest, the Guardian of Wind, and Umi, the Guardian of Water. They're experienced in hand-to-hand combat and always fight together and they fight as one. Tempest is very evasive and can move at the speed of sound, while Umi is very tactical and has more health."

"That's gonna be a little hard, fighting two at once."

"You have the means to fight them. As long as you can move faster than the speed of light, you should have no problems and break their tactics. But I would advise going after Umi."

"I have another question… How do you know them?"

"Let's just say, I knew your father, Seth Darkwind. And the struggles he went through."

"Struggles?"

"You've become very serious since Magnetin started this quest," Delphine said as she walked in. Anita was right behind her.

"And you know more than we have originally taken you for," Anita added. "Care to explain?"

"Very well, you're old enough, so I shall tell you. Before you were born, there was a scientist who goes by the name of Dr. Ian Gravestone. You remember that old man we saw at Stone Crow Town?"

"Yeah, I thought he seemed familiar. That was him?"

"He's a smart human with an IQ of 300, even for Plantian standards. No one knows how old he truly is, he may very much be immortal. Moving on, your father was actually one of his bodyguards at one point. He didn't like it too much though, claimed it to be boring, and I was his companion. After a few months or so, he and

Dr. Gravestone traveled to the Stonworth Kingdom where they met with your grandmother, the queen, and your mother, the princess. You remember?"

"All too well." Magnetin cringed a bit before having a bit of sorrow in his eyes. Delphine saw that look in his eyes again. Whatever happened must've been painful for Magnetin. Well, painful, can't even begin to describe it.

"Terrible memories, I know." Kamori sighed. "Dr. Gravestone needed some test subjects and was searching for something of value. That's when your father met your mother, Sena Stonworth, the eldest daughter, and took a great interest in her. There was no doubt that he fell in love with her. He began to slowly neglect his duties as a bodyguard to spend more time with her and eventually decided to become a royal guard for the princess, so he can protect her himself. But as soon as he did, she was taken away by someone, your father confronted, defeated it and rescued your mother. It appears that your mother also loved your father as well and decided to be wed.

"A month had passed and Sena was pregnant with their first child, you. A few weeks before you were hatched, however, she was taken away again and Seth followed. Turns out that Dr. Gravestone was behind it as they led Seth to one of his old labs. Before Seth could storm in, I warned him and told him that they're only after the baby and won't kill Sena just yet. Seth couldn't just leave his wife and newly born child, but I told him that he'll need to become stronger. And by stronger, he needed to become a Dragon Knight, I brought him to the cave in the mountains and he eventually became a Dragon Knight in one short month. It was hard, but he was determined to save her and you. After the final test, he then set off to save Sena and you, and she was only a few hours in labor. I didn't see what happened inside myself, as I was waiting on a tree branch outside.

"After waiting for a few hours, I began to worry. Then I heard the alarms sounding as Seth and Sena came out together with you in her arms. They were being chased by some soldiers. Sena tripped and almost fell as she dropped you as well, but Seth quickly caught her and you in time. Sena begged for him to leave her as her leg was sprained and only slowed them down, Seth, regrettably, did so. He took you to a place where you would be safe for the time being. He then set off to save his wife, but when he got there, it was too late for her as she had died. Seth decided to settle the score with Dr. Gravestone and told me to find you and look after you. He was never to be seen or heard from again. So I've been told."

"Wow…" Anita managed to say.

That's not everything, though, is it? Magnetin sat in silence, noticing that there were several holes in Kamori's story, but suspected since he was his father's companion, there were probably some details he didn't know about.

"It's a lot to take in, I know. But you're old enough to decide for yourself, Magnetin," Kamori said.

"I'll take the fight to Dr. Gravestone, eventually." Magnetin had a stern look on his face. "Right now, I'm not strong enough to face him yet."

"Yeah. We should take it one step at a time before we do anything else."

"But with that aside, Magnetin's a prince then," Delphine said.

"It never came up until now," Magnetin said, admitting the truth, "but yes, I am the Draconian Prince."

"Who'd thunk it?" Anita said with a shrug.

"We're about to set sail," Cinghiale said as he entered the door. "It's gonna get rough, so it's best if you stay below deck and wear life vests, we wouldn't want anything happening to you."

"What about you guys?"

"As long as we follow the direction the wind is going, we'll use it to push us in more. And don't worry, you're dealing with the finest men this crew has to offer as we've faced storms when the wind was blowing at 100 mph and raining heavily for hours."

"Don't get cocky." Anita pointed out. Cinghiale chuckled before he left the room and walked to the above deck. After securing everything, they were off. After sailing for thirty minutes or so, it wasn't as bad with the winds and the waves. But they slowly began to pick up the closer they got. Magnetin walked onto the deck as he saw Cinghiale was at the ship's steering wheel.

Andrew and Andrea watched as the ship sailed out of sight, hoping that they had a safe journey. Andrea then looked off into the skies and decided on what she needed to do.

"Keep it steady, Cinghiale. The ocean's getting violent." The captain cautioned.

"Yes, sir," Cinghiale said, tightening his grip and seeing Magnetin. "Get below deck, my friend. This is where things get rough."

"I rather stay up here and face this trial than hiding for cover while you guys are risking your own lives."

"Like I said, I owe you for saving mine and my love life."

"Don't stop me now. I may be a whelpling, but I'm still a Draconian."

"Magnetin…" Delphine never saw this in Magnetin before.

"The trial itself is just to get through this storm, but he wants to experience it himself. It makes him stronger." Kamori stated. "It is a call to action." Delphine walked at Magnetin's side.

"Then, I'm facing it with you." Delphine had determination in her eyes. Anita walked up as well.

"So will I. We are a team after all."

"Let's get serious!" Magnetin announced to the crew his favorite catchphrase, raising his fist in the air. There was a brief moment of silence as the winds began to pick up and the waves have gotten rougher.

"Hold on to something, lads!" The captain commanded. "We're hitting rough seas! Any mishaps and we'll be pulled down and left at the mercy of the violent currents!" A wave hit the side of the starboard side of the ship causing it to rock violently, everyone grabbed onto something. Cinghiale held tight onto the steering wheel as he grit his teeth.

"We're not out of this yet!" Cinghiale called. "Here comes another!" Another wave from the port side hit the ship, causing it to shake even more. Water was coming onto the deck of the ship and washed the crew. Other than getting all wet, they were hanging on for dear life. They sailed over numerous waves as they stayed on course and used the raging winds from behind them to push them forward.

"I'm glad I made my stuff waterproof!" Anita commented after getting wet.

"How much further!?" Magnetin shouted, holding onto the railing.

"Still ways off, my friend!" Cinghiale replied, holding the ship steady with all his strength. Another wave rocked the ship, causing some of the cargo to come undone.

"Secure the cargo, men! We can't lose it!" The captain command. Some of the crewmen were on it, but the water coming onto the deck made it slippery. Cinghiale wanted to help them, but he couldn't let go of the steering wheel, the waves were too rough, and if he let go, the waves would capsize them.

"Help your friends, Cinghiale!" Magnetin said, switching to earth element and grabbed the steering wheel. "Leave the ship to me!"

"Can you handle it!?" He asked.

"Just go!" Magnetin demanded. And with that, Cinghiale released his grip on the steering wheel as Magnetin held on with all his might. He gritted his teeth as his hands began to hurt. "Good thing I'm wearing gauntlets for this!" The gauntlets were providing enough protection to hold on to the steering wheel as he used all of his strength needed to hold the ship steady and his boots kept him from falling down. Cinghiale quickly took that time to hurry to the cargo and quickly tied them down. Anita ran over to him, pulled out her newest device and shot some liquid, which was the remains of the goo monster, at the ropes, preventing them from breaking or coming undone.

"That'll keep them in place!" Anita assured.

"Say your prayers, men!" One from the crow's nest said, who ducked for cover, as the storm was getting hazardous and another giant wave was about to hit the ship. This caught Delphine's eye as she saw one of the crewmen in a daze by the cargo that flew by and hit him in the head.

Delphine ran towards the crewman and raised her shield to block the incoming wave. *I hope this works!* Delphine's shield shone a yellow light as a protective barrier formed around her and the crewman, causing the giant wave to crash into the barrier and flow around them harmlessly. Both Delphine and the crewman were safe. *It did work!* Delphine looked more determined that ever. *I'm the fairy of abjuration! I can protect this entire ship!* Delphine focused her abjuration magic and made the barrier expand until it covered the entire ship.

The entire crew thought that the expanding barrier was going to eject them, but it didn't happen as the barrier passed through them harmlessly. Thanks to this barrier, Delphine was protecting them from the storm.

"Is that coming from Delphine?" Anita asked as the storm was not affecting them as much. Magnetin felt less strain from the helm.

"We're not out of the storm just yet!" Delphine shouted as she stood firm and kept her concentration focused.

The captain looked at the crow's nest. "How much longer till we reach the eye!?"

The crewman in the crow's nest looked outward and saw that the waves were starting to calm down. "We're almost through, captain!" She shouted.

After a few minutes, the storm had calmed down and the crew took care of the dazed crewmate.

"Are you okay, Delphine?" Anita asked as she walked up to her friend.

"Whoo… That made me feel good!" Delphine sighed as she dropped the barrier as the crew saw the sun breaking through.

"We're in the eye of the storm," the relieved captain sighs. "We made it."

"LAND-HO!" The one in the crow's nest said, pointing towards a set of islands.

EPISODE 7

Guardians of Wind and Water

The ship sailed over to the islands and prepared to dock. There wasn't a harbor, but there was a cove on the main island and the water was deep enough to pull the ship and set the walkway onto a stone path.

There was a female draconian waiting with her right arm resting on her waist. She had aquamarine hair up in a bun, blue eyes, fair skin, a long tail and a small build with an average bust. She wore an aquamarine-colored gi. This was Umi Mistcaller, Guardian of Water. She stood at six foot three. Magnetin walked down the plank and looked at her.

"I take it that you're Umi? Guardian of Water?" He called out.

"Yes, and congrats on surviving our test. Me and my brother, Tempest, saw everything. Your determination to become stronger is a sight, we haven't seen someone with such since your father." Umi spoke as she turned to the ship. "And quite a sturdy vessel you found and a crew you rallied." She looks at the captain, who looks at her. "You oughta be proud of your crew, captain. Because even the sturdiest of ships fall apart without a good crew. Especially in that storm, we conjured up." She gives him a wink before turning to Delphine. "Your selflessness is a natural calling for you. Putting others before yourself and your faith in your friend is befitting a lady like yourself." She then turns to Anita. "And your resourcefulness and observation lets you plan ahead of time to help whenever the situation calls it. On behalf of me and my brother, we commend you all. But that doesn't mean you should rest yet."

"I have to fight you now."

"Follow me then. Oh, and we stopped the conjured storm, but it'll take a while before it breaks." Umi tells the captain.

"We won't be leaving anytime soon, water lass," He assures. "Me crew needs a rest."

"Captain, let me go with them. I want to see this fight," Cinghiale said.

"That's up to her."

"Can Cinghiale watch?" Magnetin asked Umi.

"Of course," Umi nodded, "your friends watched your last two fights." Cinghiale walked down the plank and towards the group as they followed Umi to the arena. It was deep in the cove, the arena had water surrounding it for a good 2 feet, and there was no roof over them. Allowing them to see the bright skies.

The group saw a male draconian meditating with his back turned to them. He had green hair tied in a single pigtail, green eyes, pale skin, a long tail and a slender yet muscular build. He wore a green gi. This was Tempest Mistcaller, Guardian of Wind. He stood at six foot six. Umi approached him.

"Is he the one?" The boy asked.

"He sure is, Tempest."

"Very well." The boy got up and turned around. "My name is Tempest, Guardian of Wind! I'm sure my sister has told you?" Magnetin nodded. "Let's begin then. It's a two-on-one battle. The victory condition is simple, just defeat either one of us, doesn't matter which. But you can't use weapons, you'll have to fight barehanded. And the rules may change throughout the course of battle." Magnetin took his sword and planted it into the ground.

"I accept those conditions." Magnetin jumps into the arena and switches to the light element.

"What kind of test is this?" Delphine asked Kamori, who was sitting on her shoulder.

"Adaptability, especially when fighting against increasing odds. It's a fact all draconians know as a means of survival."

"So you're gonna use light. We'll see who's faster than," Tempest smirked. Both he and Umi went into their battle stances. Magnetin's fingernails became sharper and harder and went into his Ryuken stance he developed as a hatchling. The light from the Sun was shining on him.

"I haven't seen that stance in ages!" Kamori grinned in delight. "Blue girl! This is gonna be a good brawl!" Before she could say anything else, Umi charged towards Magnetin while Tempest vanished into the wind. She punched Magnetin and it went right through his chest, his body vanishing into the light. Nothing more than an after-image. She quickly dodged his swipe that managed to carve through a nearby boulder. Umi kept on moving, while Tempest attacked Magnetin at sound speed. The punches and kicks both were dealing with each other were booming throughout the cove. After a while, Tempest learned that Magnetin was faster than him. In the sky, a cloud was looming over the battlefield covering half of it in shadow. Tempest and Magnetin were fighting in the center of the battlefield when the shadow of the cloud cast on. Magnetin was floating in the air as he left light speed, the shadow was disabling his use of the speed boost provided by the light element. He saw the cloud slowly breaking apart at a certain section and shined on his tail and flowed through his body, allowing him to return to light speed and move into the light. Umi came to a halt as she was punched in the face. Magnetin would have followed, but Tempest was gaining on him. The cloud slowly moved out of the area and light filled the battlefield again. Tempest lifted his sister and took her to the shadow. Magnetin tried to pursue but had to stop as Tempest dropped his sister and charged after Magnetin again. He pushed Magnetin backward. Magnetin quickly planted his feet into the ground and the boot tried to grip the ground, but at the velocity, they were going broke the ground a bit.

"So you plan on taking my sister out to win?" Tempest said, pushing his rival. "How about we change the rules? You'll now have to beat both of us!"

"And that means I get to use my sword now," Magnetin smirked.

"Blue girl, take the sword and throw it to Magnetin." Kamori advised. Delphine grabbed the sword's handle and threw it into the battlefield. Magnetin then headbutted Tempest to release his grip and reached for his sword. Seeing how the wind guardian will try to attack Magnetin if he tries to go after the water guardian, he decides to focus on Tempest first. Magnetin dashed around the arena, shooting dozens of sword beams of light at Tempest, unable to do anything but dodge or parry them. Those that missed Tempest, bounced off the cave walls and struck Umi. The beams of light shred through her clothing. This continued until lightly covered both of them. When the light faded, Tempest and Umi were lying on the arena floor and Magnetin was left standing. At that moment, two artifacts, a small windmill and a bottle of water, appeared as the twins got up.

"We lost. You're much stronger than we thought, stronger than what your father was." Umi grinned.

"Yes, perhaps the strongest we have ever fought. And it's excellent how you were able to adapt when the rules changed, for, in war, there are no rules, only life and death."

"How many times have you guys done this?" Magnetin asked.

Tempest didn't want to answer that, instead he said, "there's no need for you to concern yourself with our woes. Grasp the handle on the wind--"

"Tempest," Umi growled. "We agreed that I go first."

"Very well."

"Thank you. Take the bottle of water and drink its contents. You'll gain the water element and the leggings for your armor." Umi said. Magnetin walked over and took the bottle artifact. He pulled the cork out and began to drink the content, it had a salty taste to it which made him cringe, but he bared it for the moment. Umi's body began to turn into water and evaporate. She felt her life force slowly being drained, she eyed Cinghiale and gave a smile before saying the words: "Death is only the beginning." Umi evaporated into nothing as Magnetin drank the last of the contents. The leggings materialized on his legs, they fit Magnetin's waist nicely.

Tempest approached. "Now, let me join my sister. Grasp the handle on the windmill artifact and spin it as fast as you can. By doing so, you'll gain the wind element, and soon sprout your wings." Tempest finished. Magnetin grasped the handle and turned the Windmill of the Storms, causing the sails to turn faster and faster. Like his sister, Tempest's body began to vanish in the wind. His life force was slowly being blown away, giving a grin and saying the words: "Death is only the beginning." Tempest body finally vanished in the wind and Magnetin stopped.

He felt a pair of dragon wings sprouting out of his back, tearing the backside of his shirt in the process. Magnetin's wings were red and the inner membranes of the wings were as black as night. He gave them a try and his feet were lifted off the ground, he grinned as he saw Delphine flapping her wings and joining him. Anita turned on her jetpack and flew up as well. All three of them can fly.

"You're making progress, Magnetin," Kamori said, flying up to them. "Now you three can do air combat together."

"This should be getting interesting," Magnetin said, switching to the wind element to sense the air currents. "It'll still be a little bit before the storm breaks." He informs them. "Let's go wait at the ship." The three descend to ground level.

"That won't be necessary… Because soon you'll die in this farce of a trial." A voice said from above as the sky became darker as some clouds covered the area.

The group looked up and saw a large male draconian with a defining jawline and wielded a particular battle ax. He had no hair at all, piercing black eyes, cyan skin, a stubby tail, a pair of cyan dragon wings and a hulking build. Since he was a draconian, he wasn't wearing much armor or clothes. This was Jacob. He stood at a whopping eight feet.

"I've finally found you…" A lightning bolt came down from the residue of the storm.

EPISODE 8

Trouble's Brewing

"Who are you?" Magnetin asked, baffled by the appearance of this being.

"I wouldn't expect you to know me. This IS our first meeting," Jacob replied.

"That armor. He's a Dragon Knight as well," Kamori muttered.

"What does he want?" Cinghiale asked.

"He couldn't be thinking of…"

"You'll be dead before long, but I'll tell you my name. I'm Jacob."

"No, Jacob! You mustn't!" Kamori shouted, realizing what the draconian was trying to do. "Don't you know the consequences of attacking a Dragon Knight trainee?"

"I don't give a rat's ass, whelp! I just want to kill this guy!" Jacob drew his weapon and lunged at Magnetin. Magnetin quickly dodged and flew up.

"Whoa! Watch where you're swinging that thing! You can kill someone!" Magnetin saw Jacob chase after him, spouting his wings.

"That's the idea!" Jacob growled. He rammed his ax into the cave ceiling, breaking it off and turning it into ice. Magnetin quickly did a backflip to avoid it, but one of the shards bounced off the rock and cut Magnetin's tail. He yelped in pain as his tail began to bleed.

My tail's not regenerating… This guy's not playing! Magnetin growled, trying to go offensive. Jacob placed a barrier of sorts over the hole, preventing Magnetin from receiving help from his friends. Jacob then soars into the air and waits for Magnetin to approach. The two engaged in aerial combat. Magnetin delivered two sword slashes, which were blocked by Jacob, and a kick. Jacob countered by grabbing Magnetin's leg and unleashed an Ice Breath from his mouth. Magnetin was unable to move at all and took heavy damage from it, and his body was slightly frozen but broke out of it.

"You're still a whelp. Maybe I should have waited…" Jacob spoke. "Oh well."

"W-what is it that you want me for?"

"Simple…" Jacob lifted his arm and pointed at Magnetin. "I want you…" Magnetin stood his guard. He tried to change into another element, but he couldn't for some reason.

"To DIE!!!" Jacob asked. Rain began to fall from the sky as the battle continued, Magnetin noticed that Jacob was slower, so he used his speed to try to equal the playing field and was locked in a clash, parrying each other's attacks and ended with the two locked in a stalemate.

Jacob's ax glowed with power as it deflected Magnetin's sword, shattering it two and sliced Magnetin's side with his ax. A massive amount of blood gushed out of his stomach and onto the barrier.

"Magnetin!" Delphine cried out.

"Weak…" Jacob spoke to Magnetin. "You will never amount to anything. Not even your father." He then rips his axes out of Magnetin's stomach. The barrier is disabled as Magnetin fell down. Delphine quickly caught him in midair in her arms.

At the entrance of the tunnel, Lyndis had walked in as Cinghiale noticed her.

"Who are…" He asked as she disappeared in a gust of wind.

"Now both of you! DIE!!!" Jacob raised his ax up, ready to cut both Magnetin and Delphine, but Lyndis came in and parried with her rapier. "You!"

Lyndis didn't respond as Jacob used his ax to push her into a cliff. As she recovered, Jacob was long gone. She looks down to see Delphine holding the body of a dying Magnetin. It brought her to tears.

"No! It's too soon…" She wept.

Anita went over to her friend. "Delphine…"

"If only I can save him… Wait!" That's when an idea came to Delphine and drew her longsword. "The Savior can save lives…" She gripped the handle, had the sharp edge of the blade facing down. She then puts two fingers and thumb on the rain guard and slowly pulls them across the blade to the tip. Some writing appeared on the blade. It began to shine a light down into the area. The wound on Magnetin's lower torso closed up and healed as his eye slowly began to open up upon regaining consciousness.

"Del…phine…" Magnetin muttered.

"He's coming back to life!" Anita was amazed. After a few minutes, the light faded and Magnetin lifts his body up, groaning.

"You're alright!" Cinghiale was pleased to see his friend alive.

"Man, felt like my stomach got butchered," Magnetin placed his hand on the spot that got cut. "My tail got sliced," He grabs his tail to see that it was alright. "And I got a chill." He shivers a bit. Draconians are vulnerable to the cold, being cold-blooded creatures.

"Who was that draconian?" Anita asked.

"That was Jacob," the wind draconian answered with slight disdain. "Ah, sorry, I didn't introduce myself; I'm Lyndis Skyscorcher, the Dragon Fencer."

"Are you gonna…" Cinghiale grew concerned that she would kill Magnetin as well.

"Oh, no! I would never commit such a vile act like that!" Lyndis held her hands up disarmingly.

"Why did Jacob attack the trainee?" Delphine asked. "Isn't he a Dragon Knight?"

"Jacob isn't a Dragon Knight, he believes that by killing the trainee he could become a full-fledged Dragon Knight. But that isn't allowed so that no draconian can interfere with the trainee's trial," Kamori informed.

"There's a slight problem with that… Jacob's power far exceeds that of your typical draconian. I have no idea who can stop him. I can't, even with my speed. And you are no where the level he is, Magnetin."

"So you know who I am?"

"Oh, yes I do, Magnetin Darkwind. In fact, we've met before a while ago, but you were just a hatchling then." Lyndis then kneels. "I have no doubt in my mind, though, that Jacob would try to come after you again, I'm gonna ensure your safety. I'm not implying that you're weak, not at all. But Jacob is on a whole different level, like I said. Now stand," Lyndis stood up to her full height, "you only have halfway to go and the challenges are gonna be much tougher."

"Who's the next Guardian?"

"We should head north to Plant. The Guardians of Lightning and Ice should both be on that continent." The group was prepared to return to the ship, only to hear an explosion which shook the cove a bit and hurried.

"No!" Cinghiale cried as he saw a giant octopus monster had entangled and, at least trying to, destroy the ship with its enormous arms. Its main body had to be at least 15 feet tall.

"It's the legendary Kraken!" Delphine gasped to see the legendary sea monster.

"It's huge!" Anita was awestruck at its size.

"Tentacles… It had to be tentacles…" Lyndis cringe in disgust.

"It's dead…" Magnetin commented. It had appeared to have died, though, as its head exploded from within. The captain was lying on the ground, struggling to get back up, and brutally wounded.

"Captain!" Cinghiale hurried to his captain's side. "What happened?"

"It-it was that beast tamer…"

"Francis!" Magnetin growled. "Where did he go?"

"He's long gone… The Kraken… ate me crew… but they sacrificed themselves… by carrying gunpowder… into the foul beast's stomach…"

"Blue girl! Can you help him?"

"Savior!" Delphine performed what she did before. But nothing happened. "Why isn't it working!?"

"You can't use its power again for 12 hours. It has to recharge," Lyndis informed.

"Don't worry… blue lass… my time in this world… is done… My ship… survived… use her… to get to… where ever you need to go… and please… should you ever return to Oceanus City… Let the rest of me crew… know…" And with that, the captain's eyes rolled back into his head and died.

"Damn that mutt!!!" Anita growled.

"Why is this happening?" Delphine questioned. "Why would Francis do this!?"

"Fate is a mysterious force," Lyndis commented. "And there is always something that wants to overthrow the balance. That's why the draconians exist to maintain the balance, or at least, that's what we've been told. As for this werewolf, I wouldn't know what's going on in his mind."

"They lost their lives… Because of me?" Magnetin felt the weight of the crewmen on his shoulders now. "Let's go… I don't want their sacrifice to be in vain." Magnetin now had a determined look on his face. "The ship itself looked alright. Need to get those tentacles off, though."

It took a while, but they have cleaned the ship of the Kraken's remains, rationing whatever meat on the beast that was edible. It wasn't damaged too much. Without much delay, they began to sail off to sea again.

Arctic Tower Saga

EPISODE 9

Plant: The Futuristic City

Sailing miles away from Tropical Island on the SS Cifelli, Magnetin was sitting at the bow watching seagulls fly by. Kamori was perched on his shoulder.

"Whatcha thinkin'?" Kamori asked the Trainee.

"It's about Francis," Magnetin replied. "I know Francis and he would never hurt others just for the sake of killing me. That's not his style. He may have it in for me, but I know he's above hurting the innocent. I need to confront him and settle this, as I'm the one who put him in a hospital."

"You only did that to save Blue girl."

"I'm gonna have to tie up that loose end, though," Magnetin said. "And I have the perfect means…"

"What is it?"

"I can't say until I confront him." He takes a look at his shattered sword and sighs. "Gonna need to get a new weapon…"

Up in the crow's nest, Anita was keeping a lookout for the mainland. She yawned periodically as it was a boring job, but for the good of the group, she kept her post. She was accompanied by the Black Crow. Cinghiale was at the wheel and at his side where Delphine and Lyndis.

"So, Miss Skyscorcher," Delphine asked politely.

"Please, call me 'Lyndis'." Lyndis, like most Skyscorchers, don't like formalities too much.

"Okay, Miss Lyndis."

"Just 'Lyndis'," she chuckled.

"Lyndis," Delphine blushed as she continued. "How much do you know about Magnetin?"

"Like I said before, since he was hatched," Lyndis replied. "We draconians are a tight-knit race that keep a close eye on the trainee of that gen and monitor his or her progress."

"How many are of your gen?"

"Oh, hundreds. But for me and Magnetin, we're told, have the blood of the original legendary Dragon Knights. But we don't know how true that info is."

"I've heard that the original legendary Dragon Knights were siblings. Does that make you and Magnetin…?"

"Cousins?" Lyndis as she shook her head. "Oh, no. The whole sibling thing was misinterpreted. All draconians born from the Aeternum's ashes weren't created from its blood or anything of the sort. This gave them the ability to procreate with each other without the worry of any birth defects. Only Magnetin and I aren't. And any draconian can always tell if another was blood-related."

"How does that connect between the two of you?"

"You know of Magnetin's lineage?" Lyndis asked. To which Delphine nodded. "Very well. Let me explain to the best of my knowledge, Magnetin's grandmother is Queen Johanna Stonworth the IV, and she had one consent, deceased. Sena Stonworth, Magnetin's mother, was the only daughter of Joanna's consent, who was an Asunder like her. And neither of them had any blood relations to the grandparents of me and Draco."

"So then, shouldn't Magnetin be an Asunder? Not a Darkwind?"

"Oh, he's still very much a Darkwind," Lyndis assured. "The insides of Magnetin's wings are black as opposed to other draconians, which are the same color as their scales on their wings are. Also, Magnetin doesn't have the physical physique of Asunders are known for having. Though, I'd expect him to be a little bit taller. Most Darkwinds are about six feet tall by Magnetin's age and he's only punching five foot nine. Even I surpass him in height. But I guess it's due to malnourishment. Whelps require twice the amount of food the average humanoid needs."

"I'm sorry, I didn't know how much a draconian whelp eats," Delphine said apologetically.

"That's okay. There was no way you could have known. Fortunately, Magnetin does have a lot of magical energies within himself."

"Hey, are there more Draconian species?"

"Nope, only three: Darkwinds, Asunders, and Skyscorchers. Like I said before, Asunders have an incredible physique that compliments their toughness in body and in mind, while Skyscorchers are very lean to compliment our speed, in body and in mind. Darkwinds have more flexibility in their abilities. Our names can either be our brood or something that ties them to our element. Lavaguard, Kelvin, Mistcallers, Stonworth, and Generator are such names. All draconians have one element, which is tied to an essence of Aeternum."

"Fascinating. I also know that draconians are capable of regenerating like trolls. So, why wasn't Magnetin?"

"Jacob managed to get his hands on an exceptionally material that is harmful to us and forged it into a weapon," Lyndis stated. "The material is capable of bypassing the natural armor provided by our scales and clog up our veins momentarily. There's no official name, but we, draconians, call it dragonbane, since it harms us. I figure I'd tell you this that, since you're a dragonborn, dragonbane harms you as well." Lyndis then wanted to change the subject. "Now that I've indulged your curiosities, perhaps you can indulge mine. Why are you with Magnetin? Trainee usually does this trial alone." Delphine had a serious, but concerning look on her face.

"Magnetin is in turmoil, something happened to him when I first met him."

"The only one who can confront it is Magnetin."

"I know that," Delphine nodded, "but I want to be there for him."

Anita began to feel a chill and tried to warm herself. The black crow cawed and flew off. Anita saw it fly ahead of them and saw a city in the distance.

"LAND!!!" Anita announced, which caused everyone to look ahead of the ship. Anita held a scope to see Plant. "It's Plant!"

"How long till we reach it?"

"We're still ways off, but about 30 minutes if we keep at this speed." At that moment, a seagull wearing a postman's hat and carrying a bag around its neck.

"I have mail for a Mister Magnetin Darkwind," the postman seagull said. The postman's hat was a magic item that allowed the wearer, the seagull in this case, to comprehend language and speak. Magnetin got up and approached.

"That's me. Who's it from?"

"From a Miss Carrie Fieldmouse."

"Carrie? How much?"

"5 silver. 4 for the mail, 1 for me." Magnetin reaches into his pocket and took out 5 silver, the seagull grabbed them with its beak and place them in the bag. It took out the letter.

"Thanks." Magnetin takes the letter and the seagull Postman flew off. Magnetin looks at the letter as he proceeds to open it.

"'Hey, Magnetin, I've heard from the twins that you have left the city to go on this quest. Good luck to you and don't worry about Oceanus, me and Lauren have things covered here. I'm worried about Francis and his obsession with, you might get him killed. Please, whatever you do, bring him back safely. Hugs and kisses from the sexy wererat, Carrie Fieldmouse.'" Magnetin stopped as he got finished reading the letter. "Good Ol' Carrie..." Magnetin laughed as he knew how much Carrie cared for Francis as the trio were last of the members of their old gang back in Stonworth as a band of misfits, though, Magnetin didn't really know much about them at that point. *I'll bring him back, Carrie...*

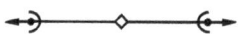

After half an hour of sailing, our heroes finally reached Plant. Cinghiale had docked the ship next to the harbor.

"What's our course of action?" Anita asked.

"Find the Metallic Tower," Lyndis replied. "The Guardian of Lightning should be there."

"Everything on my ship is secured," Cinghiale informed everyone.

"Won't anyone come to steal your cargo or damage the ship?" Delphine asked.

"Don't worry. All of our ships have an enchanted spell that makes them impervious to all forms of damage when any of the crew members aren't on board. And those who aren't guests or crew members will be put to sleep long enough for the police to come."

"What about repairs?"

"I asked the mechanics and shipwrights here to look into it. And might as well invest in some upgrades."

"Man, this place is like a maze." Magnetin looked and saw all of the skyscrapers.

"Indeed, one could get lost here." Anita nodded. She felt like she was here before. "But as long as we are on the main roads, we should be fine." The group stood along the moving sidewalks inside a glass tunnel, they saw a variety of vehicles flying overhead as well as some children hovering by on hoverboards and hover skates. Upon arriving at the plaza, some of the people were wearing gas masks, and heavily clothed and were smaller compared to the group.

"That's right. Plantians are physically weak humans, they have a hard time breathing the air and must use a mask to help filter the air. Only a very few Plantians have overcome those weaknesses, but are still frail. Plantians are really scientifically advanced." Delphine nodded.

"My crew helps distribute their technology across Earth, in order to help with innovation."

"So who runs this city?" Magnetin asked.

"Dr. Ian Gravestone," Lyndis replied. Magnetin's face became stern when he heard that name. "Something wrong?"

"I'll tell you later, Lyndis. Anyway, we should get going."

"The Guardians of Lightning and Ice are on this continent. The lightning guardian is located in the northeast. Her name's Fulmina and she should be there waiting for us." Taking one of the moving sidewalks, they reached the entrance of the city. Anita took out her truck capsule, pressed the button and threw it a few feet away from her. It exploded into a cloud of smoke, revealing the truck in perfect shape. Anita hopped into the driver's seat and started the engine.

"It's still working fine."

"Think you can do that capsule thingy for one of our ships?" Cinghiale asked.

"Depends on how the ship is made," Anita replied. Lyndis and Delphine got into the passenger seat while Magnetin, with Kamori, and Cinghiale rode in the back. They drove off.

"A fine achievement in technology, Miss Lastum," Lyndis commented. "Portable and innovative. I must ask, how were you able to reduce its size to a capsule?"

"You can call me 'Anita'. I had originally developed a chemical design to shrink something it touches, but I couldn't make it have the shrunken object grown to its original size. You could imagine the number of problems that can ensue. That's when I decided to make a mechanism that holds the same properties and functions but will also make the object shrink. All I have to do is install it. That's why it won't work on ships like what Cinghiale's crew use, they're very old fashion."

"Then why is it in the shape of a capsule and what does it look like inside?" Delphine asked.

"The capsule design allows it to be placed on your belt, in your pocket and other places. I don't know how it looks on the inside, but there's supposed to be some form of material used to protect the object from harm as well as shock absorption."

"How long till we reach the Tower?" Magnetin asked.

"We should be there in about 10 minutes at this speed." Lyndis estimated. "Though, I can get there in 10 seconds." She laughed.

EPISODE 10

Crumbling Tower

In the distance, our group sees a giant tower surrounded by a lightning storm.

"That's the Metallic Tower. It's designed by Plantians to attract lightning storms to power their machines during the Mad War. On top of the tower are lightning rods which store electricity in a large generator and send it through the Plant. The lightning storm never dissipates as it draws all of them from around Earth." Lyndis explained.

"What's the trial here?" Magnetin asked.

"Get to the top of the tower while avoiding the lightning bolts." As the group reaches closer to the tower, they see someone standing in front of the entrance.

"Oh, no…" Delphine muttered as she recognized the person to be none other than Francis. Cinghiale was ready to go over there and punch Francis' lights out.

"That mangy mutt!" Cinghiale growled.

"Hey, cool it," Magnetin advised as the truck stopped.

"I've been waiting for you, Magnetin Darkwind, it's time that we settled this." Magnetin jumped off the truck and landed a few feet in front of Francis. "You know this was coming, and I'm going to enjoy this."

"Francis, before we start, can I ask you something? Even though, I may already know the answer…" Magnetin spoke. "Why are you so obsessed with me? To defeat me in combat. What do you gain out of it?"

"What I gain is the satisfaction of beating your skull in, just like how you almost did with mine. I have the scars to prove it."

"But you've endangered and, even, killed innocent people! Don't you have a sense of remorse!?" Magnetin said he knew Francis wouldn't do so, but was trying to goad him into an answer. Francis raised a brow.

"What are you trying to play me for!? A fool!? I'd never endanger nor kill people! Even if it meant to defeat you! That goes against my code!" Francis retorted as he knew what was being said about him was false.

"You'd unleashed a horde of monsters in Oceanus City and killed Cinghiale's crew a day or so ago!"

"Bullshit! The only attacks I made at you were that tree monster and near those ruins, away from any civilization. Afterward, I turned back to Oceanus City as I managed to tame a large whale and swam to Plant. There I planned on taming the strongest land monster that resigns on this continent: The Behemoth. It took a while, but I finally managed. Behold the fruit of my labor and proof of my innocence!" The earth began to shake as a giant monster came up from behind the tower. It easily had to be twenty feet long. "I knew that you'd be coming to this continent, so I decided to be one step ahead of you."

"The Legendary Behemoth!" Lyndis gasped at the monster's size. "He's telling the truth. Think about it. It does take a few days to tame it and considering the distance to get here, the time and chain of events: There's no way for Francis to do all that in that short of a time frame."

"So, if you were here, then who was the one who committed those crimes," Magnetin asked his arch rival.

"Not sure, but I know one thing:" Francis pointed his finger at Magnetin. "No one defeats you, or kills you, but me! And once I do, I'll find this faker who's trying to frame me and rip them to shreds!" Francis turned to the Behemoth. "Behemoth! Stomp him flat!" The Behemoth, however, didn't move. "What? Don't you understand my language!? Kill that red lizard!"

"Draconian, not lizard! I don't do that tongue thing!"

"Do you not hear my command!?" Suddenly, the Behemoth raised its paw and slammed down on Francis, who managed to dodge it. "What the fuck's a matter with you!?"

"What's this about?" Anita pondered. The beast was acting against its tamer, this is unheard of, especially for Francis. Seeing the beast about to lunge at the group, Anita quickly returns the truck to its capsule form as everyone runs out of the way. Delphine caught something in her eyes under the Behemoth's horn as it passed her. It was some kind of a device.

"There's something under its left horn!"

Anita took a close look and saw it: "It's some kind of receiver, I saw that on the Kraken as well when we cleaned up its remains!"

"Whatever it is, it must be interfering with my taming powers," Francis growled.

"I don't think it was under your command at all," Lyndis stated. "It takes weeks to tame a Behemoth, while that device is sending signals to its brain. Even it is not controlling its own actions."

"What do we do!?" Cinghiale asked. "This beast is very powerful!"

"Into the tower!" Magnetin issued. Everyone, except for Francis, followed. "Francis, come on!" The werewolf compelled himself to follow as the Behemoth gave chase. Up and up and up they climbed the long staircase. The Behemoth jumped onto the railing, using them to climb as the steps were too small for it. The group took great care to dodge the lightning bolts that came down. The stairs behind them began to cripple from the Behemoth's weight and collapsed. Ways up, the Behemoth caught up and used one of its horns to destroy a part of the stairs the group was trying to run to, leaving a hole and causing some debris to fall.

"Hole!" Magnetin, Delphine, and Lyndis all flew over the gap as Anita fired at the beast to fend it off a bit.

"Back, you foul beast!" This, however, was making the beast angry. Francis ran along the wall and Cinghiale took out his grappling hook and swung across. However, parts of the platform Cinghiale landed on soon crippled just as Francis made his jump. Which fell apart as the werewolf landed, Magnetin quickly reacted and grabbed Francis' hand at the last possible second.

"Hang on, Francis." Magnetin groaned as he pulled the werewolf to safety. Francis was shocked that the one person who he wants to kill, saves him from certain doom.

"Gust!" Lyndis summoned a gust of wind to force the beast to lose its grip for a second, giving Anita enough time to fly over the gap, just as the Behemoth destroyed the platform she was on and threw an explosive into the beast's mouth. Upon explosion, its lower body was completely blown off. It roared from the immense pain as its blood fell out of its wound.

"Eww... How vile..." Delphine turned her head in disgust. Lyndis saw the exit at the top of the stairs.

"We're almost there! Just a little more!" The group hurried as they exited the tower interior and found themselves on top of it.

"We... We made it?" Cinghiale asked as he panted. Suddenly, the Behemoth rammed its head through the roof of the tower.

"Not by a long shot. Fuck!" Francis cursed. There was a bit of rain coming down as the Behemoth turned its head to the group, with nowhere left to run. At that moment, purple lightning bolts began to strike the Behemoth's horns, over and over and over again, electrocuting it to death. It lets out a death cry as its charred body falls onto the roof. Now that the danger was over, our group took this time to catch their breath. Anita approached the deceased Behemoth and pulled out the device in the shape of a dart.

"This is Plantian technology." She examined it. She decided to keep it for evidence.

"Cinghiale!" Magnetin exclaimed as the orc picked up Francis, by the collar.

"See? Your obsession almost got us killed!" The Orcish Sailor yelled.

"Wanna make something of it, orc!?" The werewolf retorted. "Put me down!" Magnetin got in and separated the two. Francis was surprised for Magnetin to come to his aid again.

"Calm down! Both of you!" Cinghiale snorted as he walked the other way. Anita walked over.

"Listen, I know you're upset about your crew. But we know that Francis wasn't the murderer." Anita tried to calm the orc down. He was still sour. "Please, don't do anything rash." Anita tended to the orc while Magnetin and Delphine confronted Francis.

"Why? Why did you save me? From that fall and from that orc?" Francis demanded to know. Magnetin took out the letter Carrie sent him.

"This is from Carrie." Magnetin presented. Francis took and read the letter. As he read it, regret began to fill his eyes.

"Carrie… After all this time…"

"You may not know this Francis, but it seems Carrie cares about you a lot."

"What have I been doing? My vendetta blinded me to what's really important to me." For once in his life, Francis was ashamed of himself. Lyndis felt out of place as Magnetin and Delphine comfort the werewolf.

"Listen, everything's gonna be alright," Delphine assured, patting Francis on the shoulder. She proceeded to scratch him from behind the ear. Like any canine, Francis enjoyed it as his tail wagged.

"Delphine… I'm sorry for when I scared you."

"No, it was my fault when I dropped the bouquet and you stepped on it." The three took their time to reconcile. Anita smiled while Cinghiale, however, was the opposite towards the werewolf. Suddenly, bolts of lightning began to thunder loudly.

EPISODE 11

Guardian of Lightning

"The Guardian of Lightning is upon us," Lyndis said, looking up at the clouds. "Look sharp." A bolt of purple lightning zapped down and struck at the center of the tower.

A female draconian materialized from the electrons. She had black hair, purple eyes, dark skin, a very long tail, a pair of purple dragon wings and a slender build with an average bust. She wore dark purple leather armor. This was Fulmina Sparkstrike, and strapped to her waist were a pair of shortswords. She stood at six foot six.

"I heard you can make people from tissues, but electrons?" Francis commented as he saw this woman's entrance.

"Our bodies are made up of atoms," Anita said, "so why not?"

"Welcome. I congratulate you on surviving the tower and escaping that beast, though I didn't plan for that. I am Fulmina Sparkstrike, Guardian of Lightning." She had parts of her scarf over her mouth to hide her face.

"You're the one who struck the Behemoth down, aren't you?"

"Indeed, I am. The beast would have died from lack of blood eventually, though. I decided to end its life sooner."

"You must be a Dragon Rogue, judging from your outfit. But why purple?" Anita asked.

"Only white, yellow, green and purple are commonly used for lightning coloration, and the other colors are too bright considering my line of work. So I went with dark purple."

"Fair enough."

"Climbing the tower was meant to be an endurance test. But considering what transpired, I shall allow this." Fulmina motioned over to the arena. "Now, young Darkwind, let us begin."

Before Magnetin stepped up, he looked towards Lyndis. "How should I combat Fulmina?"

"Her element is lightning. But her true power comes from an exposure to electrons in the area, which allows her to move at the speed of light."

"Don't think I can use the light element in this?"

"No, the clouds above us are blocking sunlight. Even with the light coming from the lightning bolts would only last for a split-second. The wind, while fast, is unable to keep up. And be wary when you use water, it may do you more harm than help."

"So the only option is earth."

"Yes, you can neutralize the electrons. Negating her attacks. But you won't be able to catch her."

"A tough one." Magnetin nodded as he stepped into the arena. *I'm gonna have to switch between elements in this fight.* Magnetin started in the light element and plans to switch between it, earth, wind and water. The two stood as a bolt of lightning came down, both of them disappeared into light speed for a split-second. Magnetin quickly used the time he had to quickly get himself into range as he summoned Arrows of Truth. Rays of light from the sky fired down onto the arena, materializing into arrows as they landed. Fulmina quickly rolled in the air to avoid the arrows, as one managed to strike her arm. Magnetin cursed as he saw Fulmina avoid. *She's much faster than I thought...*

Fulmina looked at the wound on her arm. *He managed to strike me. You are Seth's son after all...*

The split-second ended and Magnetin left light speed and quickly switched to earth just as a lightning bolt from Fulmina struck him. The lightning bolt reveals itself to be a dart. Magnetin saw three more lightning bolts strike him, also revealed to be darts. The weapons themselves were unable to pierce the natural armor Magnetin's scales provided him and the earth element allowed him to resist lightning attacks. This made Magnetin near impervious to Fulmina's physical and lightning attacks. He also used the earth element to turn his body into stone. The problem is, he's unable to move very fast. *I need to think of something…* That's when an idea came to him.

Fulmina saw Magnetin standing motionless as she left light speed, due to the lack of electrons, and landed on the arena floor. As she walked up, a hand came up from the floor and grabbed her leg as giant roots came out to hold Fulmina in place. Magnetin shot himself out of the ground with his fist coated in metal and uppercut Fulmina in the chin as he quickly changed to wind and moved as fast as he could, changing again to water and cast Bubble, spraying millions of bubbles filled with water to trap Fulmina. She found herself unable to use her lightning attacks as they fizzled out. To finish, Magnetin cast Deluge and flooded the entire tower with water.

Lyndis reacted by using her own Bubble spell to provide air bubbles for those who couldn't breathe through the Deluge.

The water that filled the tower slowly began to pour out of the roof and drain from the interior. Fulmina was seen lying on the floor, her clothes were drenched in water. "You're really something. You manage to shift between elements and use that stone body as a decoy."

"Are you okay?" Magnetin asked.

"I've been better. Just be careful with that spell." Magnetin turned to see his friends completely drenched in water.

"I'm soaked." Delphine tried to wring some water out of her hair.

"Sorry about that, draconians can breathe underwater, so I didn't think you'd need an air bubble," Lyndis said with a sheepish grin. "Though, the air bubble doesn't keep you from getting wet either."

"I hope those bubbles weren't made of your saliva." Anita shook her jacket. Francis shook his body to dry himself, splashing water all over.

"Oh, of course not," Lyndis replied, grinning in the most nonchalant way. "What gave you that impression?" That's essentially not true. And on an unrelated note, draconians can blow bubbles of any known substance as part of a breath attack. Not just water or, as Anita suspects, saliva. Lyndis just didn't bother telling them.

Fulmina dried herself and walked Magnetin over to a handle sticking out of one of the lightning rods. "Grab hold of the handle with your hand and you shall receive the lightning element and the pauldrons for your armor." Magnetin proceeds to grasp the handle as Lyndis came up to Fulmina with a sorrowful look on her face. "Don't make that face, Lyndis. We both knew this was coming eventually."

"Did it come so soon, though?" Lyndis replied. Lightning began striking the rod and began to shock Magnetin as he was filled with electrons. Fulmina's body slowly began to static as she began to lose her physical form. "Goodbye, Fulmina."

"Take care… And don't worry… For us…" Once Magnetin was done, Fulmina's body completely broke up from all of her electrons. "Death is only… The beginning…" Lyndis looked down as Magnetin turned his head.

"What's wrong, Lyndis?"

"I never had a chance to tell you, but that was my sister," she revealed.

Magnetin felt really bad about this. It was clear that Lyndis loved her sister. "Lyndis, I…"

"Now's not the time for tears. We should get going as Kamori should be searching in the northwest for the Guardian of Ice."

"We're going to go into the Arctic…" Magnetin felt unease. "I hate the cold."

EPISODE 12

Planning, Hostilities, Confrontation

"How are we gonna go down the tower?" Cinghiale asked.

"Yes, the stairs have been destroyed by that Behemoth's rampage," Delphine remembered.

"And the Behemoth's body is blocking the doorway," Anita added.

"Well, we'll need to remove the Behemoth's carcass anyway." Magnetin nodded. "Any ideas?" Francis looked over the side and saw the ground.

"How about just push it over the side?" Francis suggests.

"A bit savage, werewolf," Cinghiale snorted.

"We can't carry that all the way down. And we have no other option. Especially once it hits Rigor Mortis."

"He's right, the body is quickly becoming stiff. This is due to all the climbing it did," Delphine said.

"Can't we use the Behemoth for food purposes?" Magnetin asked. Delphine covered her mouth with the notion.

"That's a lot of meat to carry," Francis reminded, "plus, we have no way to keep it refrigerated."

"I've been inventing my Micro Capsules with other household objects, including a freezer."

"Got it with you?"

"Yes." Anita took out her case of Micro Capsules and pulled out one, pressed the button and threw it. A large freezer appeared.

"When did you make this?" Delphine asked, raising a brow.

"Do you really want to know, Del?" Anita groaned. "I already explained it with my truck."

"What about those who don't?" Delphine asked as she gestured towards the three newcomers.

"Okay, fine…" Anita sighed. "I was making the Micro Capsules a year before I met you and Magnetin and tested it on other household objects. So far the truck was the largest thing I was able to with this technology. Now, let's store this Behemoth."

"I'm gonna skin it for clothing." Francis sharpened his claws. The group worked together to tear the Behemoth's body apart and placed the meat in the freezer.

"I cannot believe we are going to eat a Behemoth…" Delphine winced as she used her kitchen knife that she keeps on hand to cut the meat of the Behemoth's bones. She saw several of the legendary beast's organs and it made her nauseous. "I think I'm gonna be sick…"

"Better than letting it all go to waste."

"Think we could make weapons and armor out of the horns, fangs, and bones?" Magnetin asked. Most of the meat was stored in the freezer leaving its bones.

"Sure we can."

"Okay, I'm gonna need to have a new sword made."

Anita also had another storage Micro Capsule on hand to store the bones. "We're gonna have to send this to Andrew and Andrea when we get back to Plant."

"How are we gonna get down?" Cinghiale asked when they were done. "The staircase is still destroyed. No thanks to you, werewolf."

"Up yours, orc!" Francis retorted, giving the finger.

"Cool it, both of you!" Magnetin intervene. "This isn't the time to bicker!"

"Why not take the elevator?" Lyndis asked, showing a set of sliding doors revealing to be an elevator. "This elevator was used by Plantian for maintenance. This elevator operates by a traction."

"Think they might get upset?"

"Don't worry. This tower is over a millennium old and Plantians are fast engineers." Anita turned the freezer and cabinet in their capsule form as they entered the elevator and rode it down to the ground floor. On the way down, they heard the steel groan loudly as the elevator abruptly stopped a few feet off the ground level.

"What now?" Delphine groaned.

Cinghiale opened a hatch in the ceiling leading outside the elevator car. Magnetin gave Anita a boost through the hatch to see the problem.

"Anything Anita?" Lyndis asked.

"I found the problem. The motor is fried." Anita examined. Delphine looked over at a sign and saw the weight capacity limit: 900 kg.

"Um… What's our total weight in kilograms?" Delphine asked.

"Only about four hundred or so." They weren't over the weight limit.

Anita inspected the motor some more and found something in the engine. "Oh, what's this now?" She noticed some misplaced parts that should be there. "Now I see, it's been sabotaged."

"What do we do now?"

"Well, we should be fine as long as no one makes any sudden movements. Unfortunately, I don't have the parts available to fix this…" In a distance away from the tower, someone was aiming a sniper rifle at a window where the elevator car was showing and fired at it. This caused the elevator car to shake from the impact and was enough to cause the gyro to give in as the elevator plummeted down the shaft. Everyone screamed along the way down as the elevator crashed at the bottom of the shaft. Fortunately, they weren't too high off the ground and survived the fall. But, everyone was still groaning in pain as they were piled on top of each other from the impact.

"Everyone okay?" Magnetin asked.

"Define 'okay,'" Anita sarcastically said.

"Owww…" Fortunately for them, the elevator door broke open up. Everyone wobbled a bit from their recent fall.

"Get off me, smelly orc!" Francis yelled at Cinghiale, who was on top of him. This angered Cinghiale enough to grab the beast tamer by the shirt collar.

"You're mincemeat, wolf boy!" Cinghiale was ready to knock Francis' lights out.

"Alright, that's enough!" Magnetin intervenes again. Pulling the two away from each other and got in the middle. "Don't make me have to place a restraining order on both of you! I still have a lot of stuff to do and I don't need this extra headache at the moment!"

"Fine," Francis growled.

"Very well." Cinghiale snorted. The two moved as far away from each other as possible. Magnetin sighed, knowing that this wasn't going to end well…

"Anyway, we should get going. Whoever did this is desperately trying to kill us and will try again." Lyndis tried to hurry them along. Outside, Anita took out her truck capsule, pressed the button and threw it as the truck appeared once again. As everyone, safe from Francis, he didn't want to get anywhere near Cinghiale.

"I'm not riding with that orc. Who knows what he'll do to me." The beast tamer was wary.

"Francis."

"As much I want to take your word, Mag. I don't trust that orc."

"A wise policy, mutt," Cinghiale snorted. Lyndis hopped out of the passenger side and into the trunk.

"I have a better idea, Francis can sit up front and I'll sit in back," Lyndis suggested. Everyone seemed alright with that as Francis jumped into the passenger side, next to Delphine. With everything set, Anita drove off to the northwest.

"Man, what is up with that orc!?" Francis growled, but at the same time, something was eating away at him.

"Try to understand, Francis, if I may," Delphine spoke up. "Cinghiale had just lost his entire crew just recently and was angry at you for it. Which we thought was you at the time, but something seemed off."

"Well, we've already established that I'm not the one who killed his crew, nor endangered the people of Oceanus. And he loses his anger too easily. We also established that the behemoth wasn't under my control because it never was. So WHAT is his beef with me?" Delphine and Anita couldn't answer that. In the trunk, Cinghiale was stewing in his own anger.

"Calm yourself, Cinghiale," Magnetin warned. "Keep that up and you'll realize that you're always angry."

"I just can't stand that werewolf." Cinghiale was on edge about Francis.

"We've already told you the reasons that Francis is innocent."

"What guarantee do you have that the werewolf won't go and stab you when your back's turned?"

"I don't. Just give Francis some time."

"Very well. But if the mutt tries anything, my fists shall be the last thing he sees."

After driving for a while, the air slowly began to get colder the closer they got to their destination.

"Are we going the right way, Lyndis?" Anita asked.

"Yes, Kamori should be heading there himself to meet up with us."

"I haven't seen him at all since we left Plant." Delphine pondered.

"He has been acting funny ever since Magnetin started this trial." Anita noticed as well. "He knows something." Lyndis just sat in silence for a moment before changing the subject.

"Hey, Magnetin, are you gonna be okay like that? We're going up to a cold area. Draconians are cold-blooded creatures."

"As much as I don't want to…" He sighed. "What about you?"

"As a draconian drake, my scales can generate and contain body heat, allowing me to withstand absolute zero. Same with Delphine."

"Lucky for you two."

EPISODE 13

Polar Village and Guardian of Ice

An hour had passed since and snow was beginning to fall from the sky. There was a forest of Evergreen trees alongside the road which had hives of ice bees, white mushrooms, and wolves.

"Can we turn on the heater?" Francis asked as the cold was starting to get to him.

"Unfortunately, I can't. In a recent experiment, I was doing something with the engine where I can make it use hydrogen rather than fuel; much like what my jetpack runs on. However, it's drawing in the hydrogen in the area. So even if you were to turn it on, all you would get is cold air."

"Oh… But how can it use hydrogen?" Delphine asked.

"The engine draws in air through the air scoop and uses the hydrogen atoms to generate energy to the motor. The excess energy is expelled through the exhausted pipes the same way as fuel does." Anita sighed. "It's more eco-friendly than fuel is."

"We should be coming up to Polar Village in a few moments," Lyndis spoke. "I hope the Maritian (Polar Bear werebeasts) will welcome us."

"I h-hope they have a campfire…" Magnetin shivered. The truck stopped at the entrance of Polar Village with two Maritian Guards.

"Who goes there?" One of the Guards demanded.

"It is I, Lyndis Skyscorcher. We're here to see your chief about the Guardian of Ice." Lyndis said, being as formal as possible. She pulls Magnetin up. "This is Magnetin Darkwind."

"So this is the new trainee we've been waiting on?"

"Not much to look at." The other guard criticized. "He looks like he's freezing."

"I'd advise you not to judge a draconian by appearance," Lyndis suggested. Magnetin let out a sneeze, spewing out flames instead of saliva.

"Gesundheit," Delphine said.

"Okay, head down this path and you should come to our chief's hut." The group enters Polar Village and makes their way to the chief's hut. There was a warm fire in the center of the room.

They met with the Maritian Chief. He has white hair, dark brown eyes, pale skin and a bulky build. He wore an overcoat. This was Esk, and strapped to his back was a quarterstaff. He stood at the same height as Francis.

"Welcome to my village. I am called Esk." The Maritian Chief greeted. "So you two are of the Dragon Knight lineage. Your little companion came and told me of your arrival."

"Kamori was here? Where is he now?" Magnetin asked, warming up by the fire.

"He just headed to the Guardian of Ice. He was accompanied by Draco Asunder, the Dragon Berserker." Esk informed. Magnetin paused for a moment. "Did something happen?"

"That's confidential between us," Lyndis advised. "Anything that Kamori said?"

"He said that your next trial is to endure the harsh cold and take a boat to a massive iceberg of ice that never melts. Kamori and Draco should be waiting there for you with the Guardian of Ice."

"Thank you." The group met up at the entrance of the chief's hut.

"Doesn't this seem odd to you?" Anita pondered. "Why is Kamori with Draco?"

"Seems a bit suspicious," Delphine added.

"I wonder what they're up to." Cinghiale stroke his chin.

"What's this about?" Francis asked.

"Magnetin got assaulted on Tropical Island by a someone calling themselves Draco," Delphine recalled. "He killed Magnetin, but I manage to resurrect him."

"You're kidding; Magnetin getting killed?"

"I'm not invincible, Francis. I think it's better if we actually went to the Guardian of Ice and see for ourselves." Magnetin sees that as their best solution. "We just need to keep our eyes peeled." The group hurried over to the docks where a fishing boat was ready for them.

"You're Magnetin Darkwind?" One of the Maritian Fishermen asked. "Our Chief sent word to get a boat ready for you."

"T-thanks." Magnetin shivered a bit. The group carefully stepped onto the fishing boat one at a time, they sailed off to the iceberg that was slightly to the northwest of the village. Upon reaching the side of the iceberg, they got out of the boat and stepped onto the ice. Their boots prevented Magnetin and Lyndis from slipping on the ice, where the boat had ice cleats for the others. The Maritian use them when hunting on the ice. There was a thick fog covering the iceberg, obscuring their vision of two humanoids waiting on the ice. One of the figures who revealed themselves to be Draco Asunder.

The other was another male draconian. He had gray hair, black eyes and pale skin and an average build. He wore arch-mage robes. This was Zero, and he held a staff in one of his hands. He stood at six foot six.

When Magnetin saw Draco, the image of Shendu was the first thing that crossed his mind.

"You must be Magnetin Darkwind?" The arch-mage scoffed, he was really cold and bitter. "I'd expected you to be like your father, but then again, a fire draconian whelp like you can't handle the cold."

"Sorry if I f-failed to m-meet your expectations," Magnetin growled and shivered. "But f-first impressions aren't my c-concern."

"I'll bet. I am Zero, Guardian of Ice."

Magnetin sneezes. "So… You're this Draco Asunder?"

"Yes, I am." Draco nodded as he stood with his arms crossed. "And as you know by now, like Lyndis, I've known you since you were a hatchling."

"You look like the draconian who assaulted m-me on Tropical Island, were you?"

"I'm sure you mean Jacob?" The Asunder growled. "I'll deal with that bastard myself."

"Draco," Lyndis approached. "You realized that circumstances have changed right?"

"Yes. And as our law states, I will assist and protect our prince."

"How do we know that this isn't a false sense of security where you eventually kill us all?" Cinghiale was wary.

"Orc, I should say the same about you and the werewolf." Draco countered.

"He… Has a point." Francis, reluctantly, agreed.

"You actually agree with him?"

"While I don't like it myself, orc, even I know my flaws and limits."

"Hmph, the werewolf has the right approach," Draco nodded.

"I hate to butt in," Anita spoke. "Is Kamori here?"

"He left a little after you got here to Pyro Mountain," Zero informed.

"What is he up to?" Delphine pondered.

"Doesn't matter now," Zero spoke. "We have more pressing matters to attend to."

"Ye-yes." Magnetin shivers. "So, what do I have to do this time… F-for the trial?"

"Endurance against the harsh, cold climate of this iceberg," Zero announced. "How long usually depends on the trainee, for you, it's only 1 hour."

"An hour. If I don't turn into a draconic icicle, that is." Magnetin joked a bit. "Do I h-have to fight you as well?"

"No. I will be decreasing the temperature as time progresses." As Zero began Magnetin's next trial, Draco walked over to the group.

"I'd advise you to wait on the boat if you don't want to die of Hypothermia."

"Magnetin will be the one who'll die from it," Delphine angrily said. She didn't want to lose her friend. "We all know that Magnetin can't survive since he is a cold-blooded creature and he's too young."

"We draconians are much tougher than you give us credit for, fairy," Draco exclaimed. "You could stab us to death, shoot us point blank and crush every bone in our body, we'll recover our wounds quickly and come back even stronger than before."

"But even so, Zero is arguably the hardest guardian to fight due to this," Lyndis stated. "Only other ice draconians can endure this effectively."

"We should be glad it's only an hour and not a day." Francis looked onward. The group waited by the boat as temperatures began to drop dramatically. It got to a point where Anita, Francis, and Cinghiale couldn't take it and wait on the boat. Delphine, being a fairy dragonborn, could take it.

"How much longer!?" Francis demanded. The cold was getting to him.

"About 30 more minutes, give or take," Draco replied.

"How is Magnetin doing?" Delphine asked.

"He's hanging on as long as he can." Lyndis nodded. Magnetin was freezing his ass off, icicles were seen hanging off his limbs and tail as Zero decreased the temperature to the freezing point of water (32 F / 0 C) and continued with each passing second. With his body numb from coldness, ice began forming all over his body.

"I'm at -50 Celsius and the hour is almost up." Zero informed as he channeled. Magnetin tried to speak, but his numbness and the ice that formed around his jaw made him unable to.

"H-how much l-ong-er?" Francis shivered and was getting impatient. Delphine and Lyndis had icicles hanging off their bodies.

"Hey, uncle!" Draco called. "The hour is up."

Zero nodded. "Very well, you manage to endure harshest of elements." The temperature began to rise back up to -10 Celsius as Zero walked over to Magnetin, who was numb, frozen stiff and couldn't move or speak, but his mind was still sound. "Draco, come help me with this!" Draco approached the two and saw the frozen Magnetin. "You won't be able to thaw yourself here, but you must break free to obtain the ice element." Magnetin tried to figure out a way how to do so when he was still numb. He began to move his body in different directions. Slowly, but surely, the ice began to crack the more he shook his body. As the numbness went away, he could feel his flame returning as well using it to heat up his body to melt the ice, eventually, it weakens enough for Magnetin to break free of the ice.

"Grrrrrrrr… Ahhhhhhhhhhhhhh!" Magnetin shouted as he broke free. All the ice that shattered circled around Magnetin and absorbed it into the armor as it began to turn a pale blue, then a belt materialized from the ice and were placed around his waist. Zero's body began to be encased in ice.

"Draco, take care of yourself, Magnetin and Lyndis." Zero nodded. "Death is only… the beginning…" His body was fully encased in ice a few seconds later. Draco had closed his eyes for a moment of respect.

"Draco…" Magnetin muttered. His numbness went away thanks to the ice element.

"Come on." Draco turned to the Draconian Prince. "We can't be loitering around here and you have only two more elements to claim." Magnetin and Draco returned to the boat where the others had waited for them.

"Are you okay, Magnetin?" Delphine asked.

"Now I am. Why?"

"After being cold for that long, you could get sick."

"Oh, we draconians are immune to most bacteria and germs as they can't survive in our bodies," Lyndis informed. "And things we can get sick from are very rare."

"Ah, good for you. Now can we shove off!?" Francis shouted as he, Cinghiale and Anita were also frozen.

"You'll have to sail the boat. My hands are frozen." Cinghiale showed his fist as they were, indeed, frozen. The group had sailed safely back to Polar Village and made their way to the chief's hut. Magnetin and the others were warming up around the bonfire as Draco talked with Esk that they'll be leaving.

"Oh, that feels good." Magnetin sighed in relief.

"Sure, you won't stay? We'll hold a party in your honor." The Maritian Chief insisted.

"No, we need to hurry." Draco declined. "There's plenty of time to party after we're done."

"That's a shame. You're welcome anytime." Esk watched them leave as he took a look back at the iceberg as if something was calling him.

Anita had already set her truck at the gate.

"What's up?" Magnetin asked Draco. "Something's up?"

"I'll explain once we leave the village." And with that, the group drove off. Riding in the back was Magnetin, Cinghiale, Francis, and Draco. Riding up front was Anita, Delphine, and Lyndis.

"Do you mind explaining to us why the rush?" Cinghiale asked Draco.

"Something is up," Anita said to Lyndis.

"Kamori has informed me and Uncle Zero of what transpired on Tropical Island. Jacob sought to kill Magnetin and then Delphine?" Draco asked, Magnetin nodded. "I see, then the time we have is short. Wraith is planning to emerge."

"Wraith?" Anita asked.

Lyndis then spoke, "Wraith is the name of the parasite that once infected Aeternum and was the very organism his sacred fire couldn't cleanse from the Earth. The name is in reference to the influence the parasite left behind and it alone was the cause of everything that had happened, the werebeasts, the Orcish Horde, the infection of Aeternum and, even, the Mad War thereafter.

The parasite itself is currently sealed away by our ancestors, Christopher Darkwind, Hector Asunder and Julia Skysourcher, with the help of others, in a holy device called the Devil's Machine, guarded by a group of fairies." She looked to Delphine.

"Wait... my sisters are guarding that parasite!?" Delphine exclaimed.

"Yes, but I'm not sure for how long, though," Lyndis said. "Jacob is acting as an agent of Wraith."

"Why is a draconian like Jacob helping something like this Wraith?"

"Jacob has betrayed us," Draco said with venom in his tone. "He's committed some heinous acts throughout the years and is a terror to life on the Earth."

"Why's he doing this, though?" Magnetin asked. "What's his motive?"

"We don't know," Draco said, shaking his head. "And I don't care whatever excuse he has."

"My sisters…" Delphine gasped in fright. "They're in danger…"

"So, my physical state is because of that… THING!?" Francis growled.

"That's why we need to hurry." Draco finalized.

"Well, we've returned to Plant," Anita announced. The group traverses through the city to the harbor and walk onto their ship, newly designed by the Plantians. Cinghiale disarmed the ward on the ship, allowing the others to climb aboard. Anita took the opportunity to mail the Micro capsule containing parts of the Behemoth to the Cashonit Twins.

"Prepare to cast off." Cinghiale took the steering wheel as the sails dropped down. Lyndis controlled the air current to sail off to the seas.

"Where to next?" Magnetin asked.

"We need to sail to the southwest to Stonworth and then head northwest from there to Pyro Mountain," Lyndis replied.

"So we're returning to Stonworth…" Magnetin sighed with discomfort.

Shadow Flames Saga

EPISODE 14

An Unwelcoming Homecoming

It has been a day since the group sailed from Plant to the southwest. Lyndis was in the crow's nest this time with the black crow. Delphine and Anita were checking the hull for stability. While the exterior resembled an old wooden ship, the inside was mechanized thanks to Plantian Technology. This included an engine that can absorb the hydrogen in the water and then expel it out the back as it turned the propellers. This allowed the ship to sail without the need of wind.

"Looks good on my end," Delphine informed.

"Same here. Those Plantians did a good job." Anita nodded. "This is quite a feat of technology."

"It's interesting how fast the Plantians took."

"They use a similar product to my Micro-capsule, but it's not in the form of a capsule, it's a medium sized box. And it's a one-time use. Mine's is the first to be smaller and multiple usages."

"I'm beginning to wonder, Anita. Are you a Plantian?"

"No, I am an elf, Del. I thought we'd established that."

"I thought all elves were extinct!"

"Not entirely, some of us went into hiding," Anita said.

"You never told us about where you come from."

"Unfortunately, I have no memories of my birth, I just found myself waking up inside a busted capsule, completely nude, on the shore of Oceanus City. Nothing before that."

"You don't remember your parents?"

"The only thing I have to remember about them is my mother's earrings and my father's firearms. What about you? I'd never expected you to be a fairy."

"I'm not sure if I expected it myself, but at the same time, I knew I was different from everyone else. I knew since I was barely a year old while living with my foster parents." The fairy let out a deep sigh.

"Does it still hurt? With what they did to you?"

"I never accepted them as my family to begin with. No worries, though, the Oceanus justice system will take care of them now."

Anita laughed as she remembered the day when Delphine's foster family were arrested for stealing Plantian Technology, applying old, rusty and damaged parts to them and reselling them at higher prices. Delphine was fortunate enough to not be part of that family anymore. Delphine smiled herself, but deep down inside, she never had an actual family and longed for a family of her own. But now that she knows that she has six sisters and a mother, Delphine hopes to see them someday.

"By the way, do you think there's any truth to what these draconians and Dragon Knights say?" Anita asked her friend. "Kamori tells us one thing, those guardians tell us another…"

"Yes, but I've come to understand that no two people will always tell you the same thing," Delphine noted. "It all depends on what they know as a whole. And there's that assailant, Jacob, who attacked Magnetin, he said that this whole trial was a farce."

"True." Anita nodded. "But all this still hurts my brain… But then, which is the truth?"

"That's all up for you to decide." Delphine finalized. Suddenly, she began to feel slight pain all over her body, which she thought was just psychological at first, but then saw an image of a being's head that resembled her but had black hair and black eyes. Up in the newly made bridge, Cinghiale took his position as he steered the ship, happy at the new and improved SS Cifelli. Draco was on the bridge.

"My ship has never looked or performed so nicely before. I can handle the wheel with ease, especially with my strength." Cinghiale grinned with excitement. Draco just stared at the orcish sailor's amusement.

"You realize what you're getting yourself into, orc?" Draco's gruff voice brought Cinghiale back to reality. "Whoever tried to kill Magnetin will, no doubt, try again. Why are you helping when you know the risks are great?"

"Magnetin and Delphine had both managed to save my marriage. I have an immense debt to pay for both of them and neither of them could sail a ship like this. This could cost me my life, but it's a small price to pay."

"Well, let's see how long your resolve lasts, orc." Draco had witnessed others breaking long before accomplishing their goals or promises. "Those who are driven don't last long before they break."

"I have never been more serious in my life." On the bow of the ship, Magnetin and Francis were both sitting cross-legged and facing the bow. Both of them were stewing a pile of their own emotions.

"It's been a long time since Carrie, Lauren and I lived in Stonworth, the roots of our pain and suffering," Francis growled. Magnetin just sat in silence, unease at what's to come. "You okay, Mag?" Francis called Magnetin by his favorite nickname. "You've been quiet for a while."

Magnetin placed his cheek on his fist and slouched. "I wished that I would never return to this place."

"You're from Stonworth as well?" Francis asked. "I do recall hearing your name once or twice."

"I wasn't hatched in Stonworth, but I lived there… treated as a lowlife."

"You too were treated badly? Should have figured at how other people said your name so sourly as those guards scrambled. You made quite a scene."

"Don't remind me."

"Though I was amazed that you survived that explosion at the Old Stonworth Castle, there were literally no survivors."

"Be glad that you, Carrie and Lauren weren't near that either." Magnetin looked away in shame. Francis knew something terrible happened to Magnetin, but it wasn't his place to tread.

Lyndis watched the conversation from the Crow's Nest, letting out a sigh. "The only one who can face your past… your darkness, Magnetin, is yourself. None of us can intervene." She looks below to see Anita carry Delphine up a flight of stairs onto the deck, hoisting her arm over her shoulder. Anita had a rough time carrying Delphine up since Anita wasn't physically strong. Delphine looked like she was in pain and Anita brought her above deck for some fresh air. "Hey, down there! Are you two alright?" Lyndis yelled out. This alerted the others.

Anita was panting from hoisting Delphine up the stairs.

"Delphine! Anita!" Magnetin called out as he and Francis hurried over to them. On the bridge, Cinghiale put the ship on auto-sail mode as he and Draco walked out as well.

"I'll be fine." Anita gasped. "Looks like Delphine is in pain."

Both Draco and Lyndis gasped as they sensed what was happening to Delphine. "I never thought it was possible…" Lyndis gasped.

"It's true then," Draco said.

"Wait, what happened?" Francis asked as he and Magnetin helped Delphine up.

"Delphine became a dragonborn," Lyndis said. "And what she's experiencing now is a delayed reaction."

"So, she merged with Santa," Draco said.

"Care to explain what's going on?" Francis asked.

"Well, we weren't there to witness it," Lyndis said, "but it's something we draconians have wondered for the longest time: how to make dragonborns, which are other humanoids with draconian blood."

"Recently, there are two methods we found out," Draco said, "by either injecting our blood into the new host's body with our fangs or by merging with the host. Both methods start the rebirth process. Delphine was subjected to the merging method, and, by the looks of it, she has all of Santa's abilities as a light draconian, which also explains how she's a Dragon Knight as well. Or Dragon Paladin in Delphine's case."

"So she's a draconian now?" Anita asked.

"She is a fairy dragonborn," Lyndis corrected, "meaning she's just as much a fairy as she is a draconian." Lyndis turned to the mentioned paladin. "Consider yourselves fortunate for such an honor, Delphine. And you've opened a myriad of possibilities for us."

"But why did she suddenly collapse like that?" Anita asked with concern.

"I believe it has more to do with me being a fairy," Delphine suggested that possibility. ***Or was it in relation to that woman I saw?***

"How do you feel now, Del?" Anita asked her best friend.

"Much better," a happy Delphine said. "How long until we reach Stonworth?"

"Not too long," Cinghiale replied. "'Bout another half hour."

"We could get there much faster with flight," Draco commented as he stretched his wings to prove that point.

Francis growled at that comment. "I prefer to keep my feet on the ground, thank you very much."

"Hey," Lyndis whispered to the paladin, "make sure to take it easy for now, alright? Just because you are a dragonborn, doesn't mean you should exert yourself like with what you did before on this ship."

"No promises, I'm afraid," Delphine whispered back.

Magnetin looked at the distance and saw a patch of land. "There's Stonworth." Pointing over yonder, the others saw the continent in the distance. ***I wonder if they'll remember me... Hope not.***

After a half hour of sailing, Magnetin's group finally reached Stonworth and docked at a nearby port. At the port, the captain of the crew met up with Cinghiale.

"You made it, we've received word from the captain of Plant's docks."

"Plantians help repair and upgrade the ship."

"We can see. They did a fantastic job. We'll take care of your ship."

"I already armed the glyphs on the ship." With that information, the captain and crew went back to what they were doing.

"We should get moving," Lyndis spoke. At the exit of the port, they were greeted with two Stonworth royal guards and a royal messenger.

"Magnetin Darkwind?" The messenger announced to the group.

"That I am." Magnetin had an unnerving look on his face. *Are they here to arrest me?*

The messenger bowed before the Draconian Prince before he unraveled a scroll and began to read from it: "Her Majesty, Queen Johanna Stonworth, has summoned you to Stonworth Castle. The royal guard will escort you there. Your companions are invited as well."

Magnetin's expression turned to shock. *Does grandma want to see me?* "Very well."

"This way to the carriage, then." The group followed towards the carriage and proceeded to enter when one of the guards, a female human, noticed Francis and stopped him.

"Halt! The likes of him are not welcome to our services."

Francis growled. *The same old bullshit...* he thought.

"He's a companion of Magnetin Darkwind." Draco injected. This shocked the guard.

"What!? This werebeast? Preposterous!"

"It wouldn't be so preposterous when I take that polearm, shove it up your ass and turn you into a human-sicle!" Francis barked. "How'd you like that mess!?" Magnetin raised his arm to keep Francis from doing anything rash. Cinghiale approached the guard, intimidating her with his immense size.

The orcish sailor then spoke on the werewolf's behalf. "Your queen has invited the companions of Magnetin along as well. Am I right?" The guard nodded. "And Francis is a companion of Magnetin." She nodded again. "So that would allow him entry into the castle regardless of any past digressions with him."

"Indeed. And perhaps we should inform her majesty about this little delay." Anita joined in. "She wouldn't be pleased with all."

"No, no, no!" The other guard, a male draconian, became frantic. "Please forgive my trainee's rudeness. She's new at this and hasn't started her rebirth phase yet. The werewolf can come, just no funny business, alright!?" He turns to his underling. "Listen, you better watch what you say or it could be your untimely death."

"Y-yes! I'm sorry!" She apologized, realizing she was wrong. The group entered the carriage as they were off to Stonworth Castle. The carriage was being pulled by horses.

"Good Ol' Cab-driven carriage." Anita sat back, relaxing.

"Stonworth doesn't rely on technology to run their lives. Everything is run by pure muscle." Draco explained the lifestyle. "The only form of technology found here are electric lights, which are solar powered."

"So Plant is a city built on technology, Stonworth is a city built by hand, and Oceanus City is in the middle."

"Unfortunately for the people of Stonworth, they are…" Draco clears his throat. "…a bit lacking in the common sense department." Magnetin grumbled at that statement as it couldn't be truer. Francis just brooded.

They reached the Stonworth Kingdom as one of the guards sounded a horn upon sight of the carriage. The castle gates opened up as the carriage entered the courtyard.

Sitting at a desk was a large female draconian. She had short brown hair, hazel eyes, tan skin, long tail and a muscular build with a large bust. She wore a set of royal clothes, complete with a tiara and a necklace. This was Queen Johanna Stonworth, and, at full height, she stood at fifteen feet.

As she was at her desk, writing down letters and documents, Queen Johanna heard the horn. The carriage stopped at the stairway. The guards opened the carriage doors.

"Please, follow us to the guests' room." The guard gestured. Walking up the stairs, four of the group members all awed at the sheer size of the castle. Guards were posted on every corner. Most, if not all, of them, were draconians. Upon on one of the balconies, an obese boy of fifteen looked down at the group before walking away. Delphine saw this boy, but only for a split second. She felt something that was not right, though. The group waited in the guest room as a guard knocked on the door. "Sorry for the wait. Her Majesty will see you now." They followed the guard into the throne room with a giant throne, out of her studies came Queen Johanna Stonworth accompanied by a seven foot tall woman wearing a robe large enough to cover her whole body and her hood was large enough to cover her face, which appeared to be wrinkled.

All, but Magnetin, kneel down before as the eyes of Cinghiale and Francis, at first, widen in shock at the size of Queen Johanna, though, who sat on the throne that was big enough for her. The black crow flew in through the window and perched itself on Queen Johanna's shoulder. "Rise as I welcome you to my kingdom. As you know, I am Queen Johanna Stonworth and this woman beside me is my overseer." The overseer bowed. "Magnetin, it's been years and you've really grown."

"Hi, grandma." Magnetin greeted. This surprised Cinghiale and Francis when they both heard that.

"Right…" Anita sighed as she scratched the back of her head. "These two weren't privy to that info."

"Wait! You are the Queen's grandson!?" Francis was completely dumbfounded. He knows a prince. "This will be quite a story to tell to the others back in Oceanus City."

"Prince…" Cinghiale approached Magnetin while on his knees. "Your Highness, I grovel at the ground you walk on." He takes Magnetin's hand and begins to kiss it.

Magnetin pulls his hand back in embarrassment. "Stop that." Cinghiale was a bit sad.

"Smooth move, orc," Francis laughed at the orcish sailor's expense.

"Guys, please, we're in the presence of royalty!" Delphine tried to get them to stay focused.

Queen Johanna laughed a bit. "No, it's fine, Miss Lightwind. I find amusement in their antics. But yes, Magnetin Darkwind is the son of my daughter, Sena Stonworth."

"You know me?" Delphine asked with a surprised expression.

"I know of you through Father Cioccolato before his passing," the queen said. "It was saddening news when I heard of it, though."

"Excuse my rudeness, your majesty," Draco bowed. "But why have you summoned us here?"

"Yes, I summoned you because I have urgent news about something…" Queen Johanna turns her eyes slowly, but sharply, to make sure no one eavesdropped. The overseer nodded to the queen that all is well. "Troubling… I received letters from Head Scientist Dr. Ian Gravestone of Plant and President Lewis Dickens of Oceanus City." When Magnetin heard Dr. Gravestone, his expression soured a bit. Queen Johanna knew of this as she continued. "Dr. Gravestone has seen reports of several of their machinery had gone missing in the last 48 hours, one of the items included a hi-tech sniper rifle with laser targeting, two robotic sentries, Model Number: 0021 and the canine-unit, as well as a prototype mind-controlling dart."

Anita's eyes widened as she quickly pulled out the dart. "Is that prototype dart this, your majesty!?"

Queen Johanna had to lend over a bit and squint her eyes to see the dart over. "Yes, this is the exact same design as the one in the photo."

"Do you have more photos of the other items?" Anita asked.

"Here you are, miss…" Queen Johanna commanded the overseer to give a set of photos to Anita, who was enamoured by the Queen's sheer size and took the photos. "What's your name, miss?"

"Oh, Anita Lastum." She replied, coming back to reality. Queen Johanna sat straight up as Anita examined the photos. "Oh, I've seen this rifle on a holographic Television Ad while in Plant. It's said to be able to snipe a target with a trajectory of 10 miles."

Queen Johanna was astounded by Anita's technology expertise but was more interested in her surname: Lastum.

"And this model has the same posture and physical structure as a werewolf," Anita added.

"Wait, Cinghiale's captain did say that the assailant that looked like Francis acted robotic-like." Delphine remembered the captain's words.

"Okay, so if we were to gather the information we have. Someone was using this stuff to frame Francis. But not only to kill Magnetin, but Francis as well when that Behemoth attacked him." Lyndis nodded to that logic.

"But, why me?" Francis was daunted by the fact that he was being used as a pawn.

"This person must have known of your ex-vendetta on Magnetin and planned to use it to their advantage." Lyndis sees that as the viable solution.

"It is most definitely a pressing matter." Queen Johanna pondered. "Does anyone know how to use those items?"

"Only Plantian can use such a device and the models cannot be active unless someone activates their neural AI which requires someone of the top brass to transmit a code from a terminal."

"So it must be someone from Plant. I'll send a letter to Dr. Gravestone about this matter. I'd deal with this myself, but I'm afraid I have to deal with other issues in the kingdom first."

"What kind of issues?" Magnetin asked.

Queen Johanna rose from her seat and walked onto a balcony outside. "Come out here and I'll show you." As the group followed Queen Johanna to the balcony, she looked into a telescope to see some of the villagers and found something. "Look through here." Magnetin looks through to see some villagers ridiculing some werebeasts. Anita looked through her scopes.

"As you can see, the humans here have been starting ruckuses against the werebeasts for quite some time now. My guards have tried to maintain the peace, but they still continue and it keeps getting worse and worse. Quite frankly, it's irritating." Queen Johanna turned to another site. "Look there." Magnetin pointed in that direction to see more villagers actually brutally attacking werebeasts.

"My goodness!" Delphine gasped at the senseless violence.

Francis growled as it brought back bad memories for him. "Nothing's changed!" Queen Johanna could only show sympathy for the werewolf.

"Were they always like this, your majesty?" Cinghiale asked, groaning at the sight.

"No, in fact, they started this behavior approximately eighteen years ago. Shortly after my daughter's death."

"But why are these humans committing these immoral acts?" Delphine could barely watch the brutal assault. "What's compelling them?"

"I'm not sure. Though there is one theory regarding Wraith's influence. Recently, I had my guards send the werebeasts on ships overnight across the ocean in order to save them from the oppression. But if things don't start changing, it'll only get worse." As Queen Johanna said as the black crow cawed, alerting Anita to zoom in and see one of the villagers, a woman had some explosives in her hands while pinning down a male wererat.

"They have explosives!" Anita alerted the others.

"Guards!" Queen Johanna cried out to alert the guards who hurried over to the scrimmage just as Anita saw the one thing she would never do.

"That woman has lit the explosives and forced that wererat to swallow it!" Anita knew that the guards couldn't reach in time as the werebeast's lower body exploded, causing all of his entrails, blood, and bones to fly everywhere. Just the mere sight of this has been too much for Delphine as she threw up on the balcony. Lyndis patted the distorted fairy on the back.

"I'm assuming that it just got worse?" Draco bluntly asked.

The guards apprehended the villagers as the head guard, a female draconian, approached the woman who killed the wererat with severe anger on her face. "Don't look at me like that! He deserved it, don't you know!" She alleged, but by looking at the fear on the other werebeasts' faces showed that wasn't the case.

"That's it!" The head guard had enough of this vice. "Take them all to the dungeon!" She looked at the woman. "And I'll deal with you, personally!" The head guard said to her with the most intimidating stare possible. She turns to the other villagers, all showing a sour face. "Anyone else who wants to spend the night in a nice, cold dungeon cell, speak now! If not, then go home!" The head guard ordered. Slowly, one-by-one the crowd thinned, leaving only the guards, the harassers and the terrified werebeasts. One of the guards, in a sense of honor, closed the wererat's eyes and covered his body with a veil, grieving the loss.

"I'll see those villagers myself. I may have to do the unthinkable if it comes to it…" Queen Johanna sighed, seeing no other viable option available. "Magnetin, you must hurry and fulfill your trial as a Dragon Knight. You should head to Pyro Mountain, Kamori should be waiting there as well. The native volcano trolls there should help you."

The black crow cawed as it took off of Queen Johanna's shoulder and flew towards Pyro Mountain. The group starts to take their leave, but not as Queen Johanna called out to Magnetin and Delphine. "Magnetin… Miss Lightwind… can I speak with you one at a time for a moment?" She started with Magnetin.

"What's up, grandma?" Magnetin approached his grandmother.

"You have come a long way since you left on that ship, twelve years ago. Your mother and father would be proud, as I am." Queen Johanna strokes her hand through Magnetin's hair. "Petranas tir ti blame doutan ihk svabol shinalta. Coi jahus vi series di unfortunate circumstances. (Please do not blame yourself for what happened. It was a series of unfortunate circumstances.)"

Magnetin looked down in pain. "Shar, si mi still responsible… (But, I am still responsible…)"

Queen Johanna kissed Magnetin on the forehead. "Tir ti hawg kornari, sia heir. (Do not lose heart, my heir.)" They are speaking in Draconic.

The group watched from a distance. "You know, if I didn't know any better, they're almost like mother and son." Francis was astounded at Magnetin and Queen Johanna's kinship. "I'm a bit envious, actually." Cinghiale nods. Magnetin stepped back and walked inside.

"Yes, your majesty?" Delphine approached the Fourth Queen of Stonworth.

"I want to thank you for helping my grandson through his torment. He has lived a rough life as a hatchling, but I am pleased that he has become a drake. I just wish I had the foresight and freedom to help him through this. But as any mother would want,

I only wish the best for my grandson. I can't leave my kingdom, so, please, fulfill my wish."

"I will, your majesty." Delphine respectfully bowed. The group takes their leave. Outside in the courtyard, Anita reaches for her Micro-capsule.

"So you're the prince, eh?" Francis smirked. "That must have made you quite a catch for the ladies."

"Ha! Yeah, right…" Magnetin denied. "I'm no prince. Even if I were to take the throne… The people wouldn't accept me."

"That bad?" Anita asked with concern.

"You don't know the half of it." Draco and Lyndis both stood in silence. "Tir trian di wux vucot? (Do both of you know?)" Magnetin asked the two, speaking in Draconic.

"Axun. (Yes.)" Draco replied.

"Wux geou tepoha ekess ehaism coi persvek wer annyo trial. (You will have to face it in the last trial.)" Lyndis informed. "Coi ui wer ergriff idol wux shilta restore balance persvek dout kornari vur xkhat wer darastrix daron wux rigluin ekess qe. (It is the only way you can restore balance in your heart and become the Dragon Knight you need to be.)"

"Filki nakta japachi zahae coi ihk jaka. (Just keep quiet about it for now.)" Magnetin advised, in a serious tone.

"Yth geou ti visp. (We will not tell.)" Draco sternly assured. Aside from Delphine, the rest of the group were unable to understand what the three draconians were saying.

"Anyway, let's get going." Delphine was keeping the object in focus. In front of the castle gates, Anita grabbed her Trunk Micro-capsule, pressed the button and threw it. Her trusty metallic steed appeared again in a puff of smoke.

"How many times can you do that?" Francis asked.

"Since it's a beta, there are about 30 uses both ways before I have to refill the chamber for the shrinking formula. I'm just glad it keeps my truck in working condition." Anita smiled in relief that her invention didn't backfire so far. "Need to find a way to extend the uses… Maybe use less of the formula…"

"Hey, Anita," Lyndis spoke up. "What would happen if that shrinking formula were to be splashed on a creature?" Both Delphine and Anita just stood still in silence.

"Well…" Delphine croaked, "There was this one time I was helping Anita and--"

"Delphine, shut up!" Anita interrupted in embarrassment. Lyndis had a blank expression on her face when she saw the reactions on their faces. She figured out what happened, but kept her mouth shut. Magnetin turned his head away, he heard of Delphine helping Anita and when he saw the two afterward, he decided not to ask and thought that it was better not knowing.

Delphine and Lyndis were in front of Anita, while the guys all sat in the back. Upon starting the truck, several of the children had tomatoes in their hands and threw them on the driver's side of the vehicle and the windshield. The tomatoes hit the side and splattered all over the side as the tomato juice and seed slowly dripped down.

"Hey, you kids!" Anita got irritated at them. The kids just laughed and made rude gestures. "That's it!" Anita exits the driver's side and pulled out her handguns. "I'm gonna have to teach you brats a lesson!" Magnetin grabbed Anita by the arm.

"Don't fall for it." He warned. "They do that all the time, even when I was living here."

"Get out of our town with that werefreak!" One of the kids laughed.

Francis growled and sneered. "Let's get out of here before I rip the skin off their faces." He said, trying his best not to yell. Anita quickly got in and drove off as the kids taunted and jeered some more.

"This town has become influenced by Wraith…" Draco came to a conclusion.

"You know, those kids looked like the same exact ones I knew…" Magnetin pondered. "Almost like time has frozen in this town."

"That's probably Wraith's doing…" Draco muttered. "His influence over this town has put them in a perpetual state. They are forced to do the same things each passing day for eternity."

"Is there a way to save them?" Cinghiale asked, showing some concern.

"Unfortunately, the only way is to cleanse Wraith's influence, but it's gotten to a point where death is the only viable option to save them."

"I'd be more than happy to oblige." Francis sees an opportunity to get revenge on the people who made his, Lauren and Carrie's lives, as well as every other werebeasts', a living hell.

"But it may be possible that even death won't save them and they're doomed for eternity to act like this in death as they did in life. And only for Wraith to bring them back again, only much worse."

"That's tragic." Delphine couldn't help but show pity.

"Indeed. Which is why we need Magnetin to complete his trial, we can plan our next move and find a way to eliminate Wraith." Draco finalized. Magnetin sighed as he clenched his fists tightly.

EPISODE 15

Pyro Mountain

An hour or so of driving, lead our group to the base of Pyro Mountain.
"Looks like we'll have to hike up this mountain." Anita examined. "Pyro Mountain is estimated to be 36,286.25 ft tall."
"Is the Guardian at the summit?" Magnetin asked.
"He should be there," Lyndis replied.
"Don't tell me we're going to have to climb up this mountain?" Delphine groaned.
"Not necessarily." Draco looked and saw a very tall, yet lanky, humanoid with charred-black skin and red veins. He also had ivory tusks. This was a Moltenstone Troll, which are a tribe of volcano trolls. His body was mutated with some molten rock that comes from Pyro Mountain, allowing him to survive the heat and lava.
"'Ello, mon. Is one of ya be named Magnetin Darkwind?" The troll asked with an interesting manner of speaking.
"I am," Magnetin replied.
"Me be leadin' ya up Pyro Mountain, me village be within it. Me chief would like to be meetin' with ya."
"Sure. Take me to your chief." The group hiked up the mountain, following the Molten Troll closely behind. They approached a cave along the way up.

"In here." The Moltenstone Troll directed as he went in, prompting the others to follow. The deeper they went, the hotter it got.

"I hope I don't turn into a meat pie…" Cinghiale muttered out loud, wiping the sweat from his forehead. Francis' stomach growled when Cinghiale mentioned food.

"Don't say any more, orc!" Francis warned.

"Ya can chow on somethin' at me chief's place." The Troll mentioned.

"But didn't you just eat the Behemoth meat not too long ago?" Magnetin asked.

"Behemoths don't have a lot of meat on them despite their size, mostly muscle." The beast tamer recalled his biology on the legendary land beast.

"I still can't believe we ate a legendary beast." Delphine was still daunted by the fact.

"Hey, it's eat or be eaten, Angel Cakes."

"'Angel Cakes…?'" Delphine pondered at the nickname Francis just gave her.

"Whew, man. It's getting hot." Anita took off her jacket and wrapped the sleeves around her waist and tied them together.

"We're probably close to some magma. Watch your footing." Magnetin cautioned.

"How much farther?" Lyndis asked the troll.

"We be dere soon, mon." The troll recalled. Delphine looked around and saw several totems carved from stone, these totems are designed to protect Pyro Mountain from Wraith's influence to cause a volcanic eruption. A few minutes passed and the group reached the central chamber where they saw a female troll dancing around a bonfire, chanting along with fellow trolls.

This female troll had fiery red hair, glowing red eyes, soot colored skin, a tall, lanky build with a large bust. She wore what could be described as shaman robes. This was Van'jin, the head chief, and in her hands was a ritual dagger.

"Me head chief, Van'jin, is occupied at da moment. Please be givin' her a moment and best not be touchin' anythin', mon."

Magnetin walked up to a pillar and watched the chant. There was a table with a female troll laying face upon it with her eyes closed.

"We're witnessing their annual ritual to Pyro Mountain," Lyndis said as she approached Magnetin, wrapping her arm the back of his torso. "One of their people is selected as a sacrifice in order to keep their totems active and prevent an eruption. Looks like this year, it's female."

"Doesn't the sacrifice chosen have any regrets?"

"No, actually, the troll will just regenerate a new heart." The ritual reaches its end as Van'jin takes a ritual dagger, cuts open the female troll's torso, pulls out her heart and holds it into the air for all to see. The other trolls all gave one final chant as Van'jin punctured the heart with her spear and dipped it into the bonfire, burning it until it was reduced to ashes. Van'jin announced the ritual's completion by raising the head of her red-hot spear into the air which the chanters cheered.

Delphine's reactions to this were covering her mouth in shock, placing her hand over her heart and, finally, felt the sensation of heartburn. The chanters had all left the area, leaving Van'jin by herself as the sacrificed troll was slowly getting back up after her heart had regenerated.

"Pyro Mountain has been sedated," the head chief said to the troll, "ya serve the tribe well, sista." The troll nodded as she was helped up and let away.

Van'jin then turned to the group once everything was done. "Welcome to me humble home, Dragon Knights and visitors. As you may already be knowing, me be Van'jin, head chief of da Moltenstone Trolls. Me apologized for you having to witness our ritual, but be understanding dat we mean no harm as me tribe served to protect Earth from Wraith's influence to cause Pyro Mountain to erupt."

"So what do you want to see me for?" Magnetin asked.

"Me suppose to be escorting you to Cinder Lavaguard, located in the crater of the mountain."

"You know we're going to have to hike all the way up, right?" Delphine hoped they didn't have to.

"You know, you can just fly up." Anita pointed out.

"Oh, yeah. And have to fight against gravity."

"We have a special means of transportation," Van'jin informed as she walked up to a particular totem pole. "Over here, mon." The group gathered in close proximity to the totem pole. Van'jin began to chant and dance around, the area began to change slightly until the group realized that the interior of a building was replaced with a cave and the totem they were in front of was the same in design but was a different totem. The cave seemed a bit small as Cinghiale and Draco had a hard time standing up to their full height and needed to bend their knees a bit.

"How about warning us next time we teleport to a place with limited space, huh!?" Cinghiale snorted.

"So you used teleportation?" Anita asked, astounded. "Even Plantians haven't perfected this means of transportation yet. It was meant to have an object travel through cyberspace to a destination. But most experiments either end up in having the test objects lost in cyberspace or worse. No reports of deaths while testing it. They had to scrap it for a while after repeated failed attempts."

"Perhaps there are some things science cannot reach yet," Lyndis giggled.

"Hey, Plantian technology is nothing to laugh at. They made scientific achievements that improved lives all over Earth." Anita defended the Plantian's success. "And my favorite bubble gum comes from them, too, Missy. Speaking of which, I haven't had gum in a while…"

"We be at da summit," Van'jin informed them. "Lavaguard be waiting ahead."

"He has my element…" Magnetin muttered. He could feel the flames of adrenaline igniting from within his heart. "I'm gonna enjoy this." He followed the path out of the cave onto the very peak of Pyro Mountain.

"And we shall watch from the sidelines, like usual," Francis grumbled as he wanted some action.

Back with the Cashonit Twins, Andrea had decided on traveling to the cave where Magnetin had his earth trial with Rex and collected his greataxe. She spent the last few days gathering all of the provisions she needed.

"Potions, check. Rations, check. Sleeping bag, check. Waterskins, check." Andrea said as she went down the list. "It's going to be quite the travel to get to that cavern again. I hope I got enough."

A knock was heard at her door and the blacksmith turned to see her brother. "Got everything, sis?"

"Should be everything," Andrea nodded. "It's going to be a long trip as I don't have Anita to take me there."

"You sure about this?" Andrew asked sincerely. "Once you turn, there's no going back."

"I'm sure."

"Well, then, I might as well go along with you," Andrew said.

"But what about the shop?" Andrea asked. Their father was still missing, so no one would be around to maintain the shop.

"While cliché, family and friends are more important than any gold," Andrew nodded as he was committed to Andrea's plight.

"Thanks, Andrew," Andrea smiled. And with that, the Cashonit Twins set off to the Searing Desert.

EPISODE 16

Guardian of Fire

Magnetin passes a tree growing out the side of the volcano. On its branches where the black crow and Kamori, for once.

"Kamori?" Magnetin had a stern look on his face as he marched through a cave leading into the crater. He greeted with an immense increase in temperature as he walked towards the edge and looked up to see the top of the volcano with smoke rising out of it. Looking down, he sees a pool of lava. "Some people say that lava is a planet's blood and the core is its heart." He theorized. In the center of the pool of lava, there was an arena with a man kneeling down and the mere sight got Magnetin's adrenaline to raise. He sprouted his wing and glided down as the others approached the edge.

The man standing in the center was a male draconian. He had fiery red hair, fiery red eyes, tanned skin, a pair of red dragon wings, a long tail and an athletic build. He wore fiery red chainmail. This was Cinder Lavaguard, the Guardian of Fire, and in his hand was a spear. He stood at seven feet.

Cinder stood as Magnetin landed onto the arena, holding a spear in his right hand. "Looks like you've finally made it!" Cinder acted genuinely glad to see Magnetin inside a volcano. He placed his hand on his forehead as if he had forgotten something. "Oh, what a terrible host I have been. I forgot the food, drinks and hello, draconian babes! We were gonna dance the night away and have a dip in some nice hot lava for some TLC and then some." Magnetin seemed unsure as to how to act toward Cinder's mannerisms. "Oh, well, there's always next time. Ma-a-a-aybe I should tell the girls to come early so we can jump straight in and just do it while singing 'Amore.'"

"Um… Excuse me?" Magnetin spoke up.

"Yes?" Cinder came up close to Magnetin, causing the Draconian Prince to walk back a bit. "What do you want? Can't you see I'm busy."

Magnetin cleared his throat. "I'm here to fight you for the fire element?"

"Oh! Right, right, right!" Cinder then takes out a scroll and reads it. "Let me see… Ah! 'I thank you for climbing up Pyro Mountain, facing perilous obstacles and dangerous creatures along the way and growing ever weary to reach the top… My name is Cinder Lavaguard… yadda-yadda-yadda…'"

Delphine whispered to Lyndis while covering her mouth behind her hand. "Should we tell him about the totem?"

Lyndis proceeds to whisper back to Delphine: "Nah. Let him be."

"This stuff is giving me a headache…" Anita groaned as she scratched the back of her head.

Cinder continued to read before throwing the scroll into the lava which burst into flames. "AHHHH! Too much dialogue! So how about we get to the meat of this, eh?" Cinder ready his spear and took his battle stance. Magnetin brandishes his claws and took up his Ryuken style again since he didn't have a weapon to fight with.

They started by charging at each other with Cinder thrusting with his spear, but Magnetin used his right claw to parry it to the left and swung his left claw up. Cinder quickly blocked this with his spear but was lifted into the air. He used this momentum to aim the blunt end of the spear to whack Magnetin in the chin. Magnetin's tail had anchored itself into the arena and pulled himself away to avoid the strike and flipped back, trying to kick Cinder in the thigh and actually landed. This caused Cinder to flip back, but regained his balance and landed, feeling the pain in his thigh.

"Nice counter." Cinder was impressed with his combatant. He quickly charged again but wasn't going for a thrust like before only this time as Magnetin grabbed the spear, but was forced into the lava along with Cinder.

"Magnetin!" Cinghiale exclaimed, as he and Francis feared the worst.

"Fret not. For draconians, lava is like water to us." Draco reminded her.

"And he is a fire draconian on top of that," Lyndis added.

"Volcano trolls can survive in lava and heat, but not in water and coldness," Van'jin added.

In the lava, Magnetin and Cinder continued their struggle while not letting the other one have an opportunity to strike. Magnetin's feet reached the bottom of the lava pool. Allowing him to kick off and use the momentum to deliver a claw slash that almost scratch Cinder's face, who tilted his head to the side only to be punched in the face.

The force launched Cinder out of the lava pool and back onto the arena. Magnetin followed by jumping out. Cinder had some blood leaking out of the side of his mouth. "Very Impressive. Shall we move to the finale?" Cinder performed a jump that shot him up into the skies at an incredible velocity. He looked like a comet flying.

Magnetin saw that there was no way to avoid this attack, so he quickly jumped up as well and used his wings to gain as much altitude as he could… until Cinder quickly descend faster than Magnetin could see, piercing his spear into Magnetin's torso, barely missing his heart and pendant. Both plummeted back into the crater and crashed straight into the arena. Magnetin was writhing in pain as Cinder removed his spear.

"Magnetin!" Delphine gasped to see her friend in sheer pain. The others all looked worried for the trainee. Magnetin was holding his chest in pain as blood dripped.

"Your scales haven't matured enough to withstand my attack and pierced right through. You're still just a whelp." Cinder criticized, his demeanor has changed. "Come back in two years time when you've become a drake." Magnetin struggled to get back on his feet.

"Should we help him?" Anita asked.

"ALL OF YOU, STAY WHERE YOU ARE!!!" Magnetin yelled as loud as he could. "I may be a whelp… But I'm not done yet!"

"He's alright." Kamori nodded.

"It appears that your heart's on fire, yet you're willing to fight with a hole in your chest."

"Maybe you… shouldn't miss my heart next time!" The wound on Magnetin's chest healed.

Cinder jumped up into the skies again as Magnetin followed. As Cinder reached the peak of his jump, ready to descend, Magnetin had changed to the Heavens armor using the light from the sun to speed himself up to punch Cinder in the face and claw him about ten times. Magnetin then followed by grabbing Cinder and began to do a number of high-speed loops to daze Cinder and dive back down, working with gravity to increase speed and slamming straight into the crater and onto the arena, with enough force to cause the lava to splash up. Delphine, Draco and Lyndis kept the group safe from the lava.

Cinder's spear flew out of the lava and landed near Van'jin.

As the debris cleared, the arena broke apart, causing it to sink into the lava. Cinder was floating in the lava without a care in the world.

"So where are these Draconian Babes that you mentioned?" Magnetin smirked. "You promised me."

"Unfortunate for you, you won't have much time to stay here to do that." Cinder laughed. "And unfortunate for me that I won't be around to enjoy it anymore." Cinder stood right up. "But it must be done for you to fulfill your destiny." Cinder began to concentrate as the lava began to rise up to submerge the two. Magnetin felt the lava temper his scales and a chainmail out of the lava that covered his torso. Cinder's body began to turn to charcoal as the lava began to lower, revealing Cinder's charred body and Magnetin's new chainmail and the fire element. "Death is only the beginning… Good night, everybody!" Cinder said sincerely as his head charred and his entire body slowly reduced to ashes. Magnetin sprouted his wings and flew out of the lava pool and back onto the edge. His trial was almost complete and had just one more element to go before becoming a full-fledged Dragon Knight.

"Magnetin!" Anita hurried to her friend. "How's your wound?" She looked at his torso and saw that there was no blood on it nor wound to be found. "How are you able to heal from that great of a wound so quickly?"

"We draconians are capable of regenerating our wounds quickly. Minor wounds are gone in split seconds while major wounds only take up to a day at most." Lyndis informed a bit about the biology of draconians. "So being in the lava, or around any source of heat, allowed Magnetin's wound to heal instantaneously with no scars. So far, only dragonbane can stop it."

"How are you feeling?" Kamori asked.

"Much better."

"Now the time has come for you to undergo the final trial: Umbra Cryptlurker, Guardian of Shadows."

"Her trial is a bit different than the rest, though, as you won't be fighting her. And her location is always different, but it's always the place where the trainee's most regretful moment."

Magnetin looked down. "I know where… In the ruins of the Old Stonworth Castle." He knows that the time has come. Van'jin was captivated on Cinder's spear.

"Van'jin?" Draco got her attention. "We're gonna need your teleportation to return down to ground level."

"Me be dere." Van'jin looked back at the spear shortly before heading back to the totem. The black crow went ahead by flying down to their next destination. With a tight squeeze for Cinghiale and Draco, the group teleported back to Van'jin's hut. Van'jin decided to stay as there was some business for her to attend to, leaving the group to head back out to the base of the mountain. As Anita set her vehicle up, Magnetin looks up and saw the black crow in the distance.

EPISODE 17

Guardian of Shadows

Anita drove her truck back the way they came, but made a right turn to the south as it's where the Old Stonworth Castle still stands. Much of the castle had deteriorated away, but its foundation and several of the towers still stood.

"It's as if time stopped here…" Magnetin commented as he gazed at.

"So, where is this Umbra?" Cinghiale asked.

"I'm under your nose." A voice called out. The group saw the shadow of the black crow stretch down and rise up against the wall.

"What sort of illusions is this?" Francis couldn't believe a shadow moving on its own. Cinghiale and Anita were also baffled as well.

"Be careful, Magnetin," Lyndis warned. "Not much is known about Umbra."

The shadow pointed in a direction as the black crow cawed and flew in that direction. "Follow." As Magnetin walked through the entrance, a black shadow covered it, cutting Magnetin from the others.

"Mag!" Francis called out.

"Don't touch that barrier! Magnetin has to face Umbra alone." Kamori informed the others. The group could only watch as Magnetin walked on, following the black crow down into the catacombs and through a corridor that had lit candles on the walls.

"No one has been here for years, so these candles…" Magnetin felt something brush up against his arm, causing him to look, but saw nothing there. He then felt something brush up against the base of his neck, causing him to look that way, but saw nothing again. "I know you're here."

"How perceptive of you… Yes, I am here. I am there. I am everywhere." The voice cooed and echoed through the corridor. "So you're Magnetin Darkwind. Such a strong draconian you've become. Like your father." Magnetin continued walking. "But your heart is still heavy, with such burden and regret. Poor whelp." Magnetin reached a platform in the catacombs. The walls were decorated with bones.

"Show yourself," Magnetin spoke.

He could see a shadow rising from the ground and taking the form of a very attractive woman who appeared to be the splitting image of Delphine. She had black hair, black eyes, pale skin and the curvaceous build with a big bust. She wore nothing but straps that covered her entire body from head to toe and barely contained her big bust. On her forehead was an ivory tiara and the gem was a diamond. This was Umbra Cryptlurker. She stood at seven feet.

"I am Umbra Cryptlurker, Guardian of Shadows." Umbra introduced herself.

"Quite a unique power." Magnetin was impressed. "The ability to turn your body into the shadows and blend in."

"I'm flattered. Indeed, my power is unique. But we'll dwell on that later. Right now, you must overcome your final trial by re-witnessing your past and your nightmare." Umbra held her hand out. "Come. Onto the platform with me and wrap your arm around my body." Magnetin did just that and Umbra did the same to him. The shadow draconian placed a hand on Magnetin's cheek and rubbed it firmly. "Close your eyes, and let us begin." He did so as Umbra gave the Draconian Prince a kiss on the cheek and dived into his subconscious domain.

Magnetin was sinking down into the depths of his subconscious domain until he landed onto some kind of floor.

"Magnetin, I have given life to your memories of the past," Umbra said through telepathy. The area was coated with thick, dark clouds which represent the darkness of Magnetin's heart.

Magnetin looked and saw the dark clouds forming a younger version of himself, but had a rather irritated, yet blunt look on his face.

"Everyone can just fuck off and die for all I care." The younger Magnetin said. Magnetin remembered that sentence all too well. What he was and how he acted. He remembered it.

Voices were echoing through the darkness. "It's that fucking lizard again." Magnetin knew this. A crowd of people without faces began to take form from the darkness.

"It's all because of him the princess died."

"We should hang him for murder!"

"People accuse me of things I can't control." The young Magnetin continued as more jeers came from the darkness.

"You're a worthless scum."

"You gonna run with your tail between your legs, lizard?"

"They hated me. So I hated them back." Magnetin saw images of himself stealing from shops, clothing, food, and necessities. Needless to say, Magnetin had a rough childhood and spent it as a thief and a prankster. It was his way of getting them back, to put it in nicer words. He saw an image of him stealing a bunch of fireworks and quietly placed them under a vendor's booth and set them off to start a panic. He saw another image of himself with a bucket of pink paint and placing it close to the edge of a rooftop, there were kids beneath him. He let down a line and hook with snagged into a kid's shirt, who was pushed down by one of the largest males in the group, causing the bucket to spill and drop on his head. The other kids laughed at the large boy covered in pink paint and blind by the bucket. He carefully planned out each prank and did it from the shadows, also giving himself a back up to get out of a sticky situation.

There was another where he saw a man about to eat pork but swapped it for a rotten one. The instant the man bit the rotten meat, he spit it right out, coughing and complaining to the chef. Magnetin then ate the pork.

Another image showed him having green food dye and some women enjoying a sundae, steadying his position, he used ventriloquism to distract the women long enough to get a few drops in the sundae for it to turn green. The women turned back to their sundae only to look away in disgust.

There were several times where the guards came. But Magnetin was faster than any of them as he was out like a flint.

The image then shows Magnetin in a pet shop, releasing animals from their cages. This is where he met Kamori for the first time and helped him by scaring the animals into attacking the owner as she came in. This moment where Kamori became his partner in crime. Kamori would stir up trouble, while Magnetin would set up the prank. Some involved food for them to eat, while others involved supplies.

One image showed Magnetin and Kamori sneaking into his room in the original Stonworth Castle. A woman came into his room. It wasn't Queen Johanna, but a human acolyte. She had vanilla white hair, eyes, pale skin and a voluptuous build with a big bust. This was Vaniglia, she was Magnetin's caretaker, and she looked eerily similar to Delphine, but only stood at five foot eight.

"Magnetin Darkwind! Have you gone out raising a ruckus again!? There were reports of animals being set free and attacking the pet shop owner there. She had numerous scars all across her face." Vaniglia scold, but Magnetin easily deflected it.

"Pfft… Maybe she could let them out once in a while and not have them be locked up like they're prisoners." Magnetin simply lay on his bed, stroking Kamori's back.

"This creature with you…" Vaniglia noticed Kamori. "Don't tell me you've picked up a stray…"

"For your info, I found Kamori locked up in a cage with the other animals. So I decided to keep him."

"Magnetin, you're the next heir of the Stonworth line. You need to be more considerate of your subjects and those around you."

"What's the point?" Magnetin sighed and looked out the window.

Vaniglia just sighed. "Anyway, dinner is almost ready, please dress appropriately."

"What about food for Kamori? A day of pranks left him hungry as well."

"We'll get him something to eat as well." Vaniglia left the room. Grumbling in discontent, Magnetin dress up as nicely as he could and walked to the dining hall. There were only two people present, Magnetin and Queen Johanna. The two began with an appetizer, Brushetta al Pomodoro (a tray of cured meat, tomatoes, vegetables and cheese on bread). Next dish, Magnetin had a Garden Salad while Queen Johanna had Minestra Maritata (Wedding Soup). For the entree, Magnetin had some Cheese Ravioli with Fresh Vegetables, Queen Johanna had Orecchiette (Small Ears) with Red Pepper Pesto. And for dessert, Magnetin had Pineapple Tiramisu and Queen Johanna had Panna Cotta.

"Magnetin, I've been hearing news of a rising gang in the village. Seems several werebeasts are tired of being spat on. You haven't been going near these gangs, have you?" Queen Johanna raised an eyebrow at the young draconian.

Magnetin just looked straight at her, looked at Kamori and then looked back at her. "No, first I've heard of it." Shaking his head.

"You better not. While I understand the merit of your actions and the actions of the werebeasts, I will not tolerate any harm that befalls the innocent."

"Innocent? Who's innocent? Because the villagers certainly aren't!" Magnetin retorted. This earned him a smack upside the head by Vaniglia. This didn't hurt the draconian, but it did irritate him.

"Mind your words." Vaniglia scolded.

"They blame me for things I can't control, ridiculed and jeered. I don't wish to rule over those kinds of people. They'll never accept me as a king, anyway."

"Magnetin…" Queen Johanna was at a loss for words. Magnetin finished his dessert and left the dining room. Queen Johanna sighed as Vaniglia approached her.

"Your Majesty…"

"Vaniglia please look after my grandson. I feel that something terrible is going to befall him."

"Yes, your majesty." Vaniglia bowed before leaving the dining room as well.

The next day, Magnetin and Kamori went around town to see anything about this gang of werebeasts. They were said to be in the slums. There was a fence to prevent the werebeasts and humans from fighting each other. Magnetin jumped over the fence and landed on top of a roof and continued until he saw a rally of werebeasts. Little did he know that he was being followed by Vaniglia.

They had been persecuted since their ancestors were minions of Wraith and his influence which cursed them into their feral forms. The descendants, however, inherit the bestial forms and traits into their biology rather than a curse. This ranged from wolves to cats to rats. They seemed like they were preparing for a civil war with the humans of Stonworth. Magnetin watched from the rooftops but kept low.

"Brethren! For too long we've been spat on and treated like a horrible plague by the humans! Now it's time we shape our future into our own claws, through bloodshed if need be!" The leader of this militia announced.

"Blood and thunder!" The crowd cheered.

"They're planning to go to war?" Magnetin muttered.

"Magnetin Darkwind!" He heard a recognizable voice call him below. It was Vaniglia. "You are in big trouble!"

"Vaniglia!? Did you follow me?" Magnetin asked as he jumped down.

"I should have known that you would get involved with the werebeasts."

"That's not it at all! I was just inspecting this gang and turns out they're preparing for war with the humans!"

"War!?" Vaniglia cried out. This caused several werebeasts to hear Vaniglia's cry and broke through a wooden fence.

"Hey, we got spies here!" A werecat called out to the others. Magnetin grabbed Vaniglia by the hand and both of them ran as fast as they could, but Vaniglia tripped on uneven ground and fell to the ground. This caused a sprain in her ankle.

"Come on, Vaniglia!" Magnetin tried carrying Vaniglia but wasn't strong enough to lift her, he was barely six years old and hadn't developed enough strength yet.

"Leave me and save yourself! I'll only slow you down!" Vaniglia told Magnetin to run. She couldn't bear the thought of any harm coming to Magnetin.

"No way!" He tried, but no success.

"Just go!" Vaniglia pushed him, forcing him to run back. Some werebeasts had captured Vaniglia and took her as a hostage.

"Someone help! Vaniglia has been captured by the werebeasts!" Magnetin cried out. Most of the villagers didn't care, believing it to be some prank, but the draconian guard stationed there didn't ignore.

"What is it? Werebeasts?" The guard answered the call as Magnetin ran up to him.

"Please, hurry! The werebeasts are planning for a civil war and they're gonna use Vaniglia as a hostage or kill her!"

"I'll rally the others!" The guard gave his word. But one of the villagers came across.

"You ain't seriously gonna believe this fucking lizard, are you?" The villager spat at the guard.

"I'm not even going to argue with you about that statement, human. But your families and friends are endangered! Evacuate now!" The guard sternly warned the villager, who began to argue.

"I ain't running and let some werefreak get the best of me! This has been a long time coming!" Magnetin could see that this was a waste of time and decided to head back to the werebeasts and save Vaniglia himself.

"Kamori, fly back to grandma and get help! I'll see what I can do!" He ordered his companion as Kamori flew to the castle. Magnetin quickly jumps along the rooftops, hoping that he isn't too late. He carefully sneaked through the werebeasts' lines and made it to a house where he heard voices inside.

"Are you sure it's wise for us to take a human hostage, it'll only aggravate the human's more." A werewolf with a familiar voice asked another.

"She's probably a spy sent by the humans, Francis." The familiar werewolf was, indeed, a young Francis McWolfwood.

"But I'm not a spy!" Vaniglia tried to prove otherwise.

"Silence, hostage!" The older werewolf said to Vaniglia, striking her in the head. "We're gonna launch our assault while they least expect it. Chain her to the wall and watch over her." He then kicked Vaniglia over to Francis, who caught her.

"Come quietly, human," Francis ordered. He tried not to be too rough with her as she was chained. The other werewolf left, leaving Vaniglia and Francis alone, slamming the door shut.

"Is he g-gone?" A familiar voice was heard from a female werecat cowering in the lap of a familiar female wererat.

"It's okay, Lauren," the wererat assured. The werecat was a young Lauren Tomcat and the wererat was a young Carrie Fieldmouse. Carrie got up and approached Vaniglia. "Is this the spy? She doesn't look the part?"

"I keep telling you I'm not a spy. I just came here looking for someone."

"Well, human, you picked the wrong time to come here." Francis huffed. "You're lucky I'm not like the other bloodthirsty werebeasts your kind despises."

"Well, hadn't I not been saved by the castle when I chose to go into service, I probably would have despised you," Vaniglia replied, her head was sweating in fear, not knowing what will become of her.

"Unfortunate, your fate is not for me to decide. If it were up to me, I'd let you flee from this village. I despise humans, but I won't go as far as to harm or kill an innocent or defenseless person." Francis expressed himself and his values. Vaniglia can see under Francis' rugged exterior. Suddenly, Magnetin had dropped in from above.

"Magnetin, why are you here!?" Vaniglia cried out.

"To save you what else!"

"You're that whelp that escaped." Francis loomed over the young draconian. "You got balls for coming into enemy lines and saving your friend. I like balls."

"Thanks for the compliment even though I've been treated the same way as you." Magnetin prepared a fighting stance.

"You really want to fight this hatchling, Francis?" Carrie asked the werewolf. Lauren was cowering behind Carrie from Magnetin's sudden entrance.

"Wait, don't fight!" Vaniglia begged for them to not fight. "Please, hear me out. There is a city called Oceanus just to the east across the ocean. There's a port a few miles away from this village, there are sailors who ship some goods to get there. The humans there aren't like the ones here." This information caused the trio's ears to perk up.

"How are we gonna pay to get across?" Carrie brought up the money issue.

"They usually let passengers on for free if you help them load stuff onto and off the ship. It's part of their policy."

"Why are you telling us this?" Francis grew suspicious. "This better not be some trap."

"No, I'm trying to save you three. Please, hurry."

"Francis, I say we take this human up on her offer and get out with our lives." Carrie agreed.

"Very well." Francis took out the key and unlocked Vaniglia's shackles. "My debt has been paid. Get out of here quickly, both of you." Vaniglia sees Lauren cringe in pain as she licks the back of her hand.

"Wait!" Vaniglia told them to halt.

"What now?" The trio sees Vaniglia approach Lauren, who quickly cowered behind Carrie.

"Your hand looks injured. Please let me wrap it up." Vaniglia let her hand out and had a roll of lined bandage ready. Though scared at first, Lauren placed her hand in Vaniglia's hand for her to wrap it. "The bandage will heal your wound in no time."

"T-t-thank you, miss…" Lauren replied. She never experienced such kindness before, especially from a human. The trio quickly left, leaving Magnetin and Vaniglia alone.

"I can't believe how easily you manage to persuade them," Magnetin commented.

"Thank you. Working in the castle, you pick up lots of things. But I do feel sorry for them and I wanted them a better chance at life." Vaniglia said her reasons.

"We need to get out of here as well before the other werebeasts come back."

Magnetin jumped onto the rooftop and pulled Vaniglia up, the two can see the fire blazing in the village. Magnetin had jumped over to another rooftop, but Vaniglia had a problem.

"What is it?"

"I can't jump with my ankle." Vaniglia reminded him of her sprained ankle.

Magnetin jumped back across. "Okay, then, I'll carry you." He proceeds to perform the bridal carry.

"Wait! I'm too big for you!" Vaniglia wasn't sure that this was going to work.

But that didn't stop Magnetin from lifting her in his arms, mustering all the strength he had. It was at this moment, that Magnetin began to feel his muscles grow slightly, increasing his strength and lift Vaniglia easily.

"What's happening?" Vaniglia was shocked at Magnetin's new strength.

"I'm stronger now, that's what!" Magnetin grinned as he prepared to jump. "Hang on!" He leaps onto each rooftop with ease until they reached a shack not too far from the carnage.

"Where're the guards!?" Vaniglia looked to see none of the castle guards around.

"When I went for help, one of the villagers began to argue with the guard stationed here."

"Typical…" Vaniglia sighed.

"I sent Kamori to inform Grandma." Magnetin then smelt smoke from beneath them in the shack. "Wait, isn't this shack where they store the fireworks?" Both of their faces paled with feared right as the shack had exploded, launching both Magnetin and Vaniglia into the air and landed hard on the ground a few yards away and right near where a male human and a female werecat were fighting each other.

"Are you okay, Vaniglia?" Magnetin asked as he can endure a fall like that, but a human can't.

"I should be fine, but my ankle." Vaniglia's ankle had suffered more injury from the fall, disabling her ability to walk. Magnetin tried to get up and help Vaniglia, but the two combatants ran into Magnetin as the werecat's foot pinned his body down to the ground.

"Get... off... me!" Magnetin grunted in pain, pushing his body up. The werecat noticed this and pushed her human combatant back and away from the two. He rubbed his back as the pain subsided and hurried to Vaniglia. But the human pushed and knocked the werecat into Magnetin, causing him to fall on top of Vaniglia with the werecat on top of them and being pinned by the human.

"Foul human!" The werecat spat as she tried kicking him, who rolled away to avoid the kick. The werecat got up and charged at the human, but he quickly used his shield to block her. The human took his sword and pierced the werecat in the abdomen, the pain was so severe it disoriented the werecat as the human moved his blade horizontally and sliced her in half. Vaniglia could only cover her eyes in disgust.

"Fucking Lizard, I have you now!" The human was overloaded with a killer intent towards the young draconian. Magnetin tried moving, but constantly being crushed on had left his body in agony. He prepared for the worst as he felt his body was being pushed out of the way. He opened his eyes just to see Vaniglia, who had saved him from suffering a serious cut only to get cut herself.

"Vaniglia!" Both young and old Magnetin cried out as his caretaker fell to the ground with a massive sword wound on her side, bleeding. "Vaniglia. Please, Vaniglia, get up." The young Magnetin began to shed tears.

"Magnetin," Vaniglia mustered up enough strength to speak her last words. "Please, don't despise humans. Our lives are already filled with hardships. We can do great things. So, please… find everyone a brighter future." Vaniglia coughed up blood. "Magnetin, I know… you can do it… Arrivederci, Magnetin Darkwind…" And with that, Vaniglia died in front of Magnetin's eyes.

"You, fucking lizard, see what you've done!? She's dead because of you! It's all your fault!" The villager spat venom at him. "Don't worry, I'll put you out of your misery!" The villager held the tip of his blade against the back of Magnetin's neck, proceeding to behead him.

"Y-you…" Magnetin growled as rage and anger began to rise alarmingly. The villager swung his sword only for Magnetin to catch it with just one bare hand and gave the villager the most intimidating look ever mustered. This caused the villager to become riddled with fear as Magnetin took the sword and rammed it through the villager's stomach. He then incinerates the villager with a fire breath until he was nothing but a charred skeleton.

Once that was over and done with, Magnetin walked over to the deceased Vaniglia and began to dig a hole to give her a proper burial as the fighting continued around them. Several explosions went off during the fighting, including one that shot a fireball into the air and struck the castle, crumbling a section of it down.

The older Magnetin watch the younger Magnetin bury Vaniglia's body in the ground, both of them shed tears. Queen Johanna arrived moments later, walking towards her grandson and looked at the aftermath. Magnetin had lost his childhood innocence. Rain began to fall.

Another image has Queen Johanna at the port asking one of the captains to take Magnetin with them across to Oceanus City. She sent a pigeon with a message to a priest there named Father Cioccolato, who's willing to take care of Magnetin. She saw her grandson off personally and watched as the ship sailed out of sight.

"Please be safe."

The final image has Father Cioccolato carrying Magnetin to his church in Oceanus accompanied by a young Delphine Lightwind.

This entire ordeal left Magnetin silent for years on end. Ashamed of himself and constantly running from his past. The sword Magnetin carried was the same sword that slain Vaniglia.

"In the end, it didn't matter!" Magnetin stood there in the darkness, cursing himself for letting Vaniglia perish. "In the end, I couldn't save her… And took my rage out on that villager… Damn it. Damn it! Damn it all!"

"Stop blaming yourself, Magnetin." Vaniglia's voice spoke to him. This caused Magnetin to open his eyes and see Vaniglia standing right in front of him. Magnetin ran over to hug her, but he passed right through her. "I'm sorry, but I'm no longer on this plane. I'm just a ghost now." Magnetin turned to face her. Tears were filling up in his eyes. "You've grown so much…" Vaniglia smiled. "Magnetin, I gave my life for you so that you may live on. Look around you, you already have a number of people who still love you, still alive." He began to think about all of his friends and family as his pendant began to glow with power.

"All this time… I've been running from the past… But turns out I was always trapped in the past like a prison…" Magnetin looked at his younger self. "But now… I have people to help me through it… Grandma and Kamori… Delphine and Anita… Francis and Cinghiale… Draco and Lyndis… Andrew and Andrea… Lauren and Carrie…" He began to smile as his pendant glowed brighter, with a ruby now embedded in it and causing the darkness around him to vanish.

"He's done it," Umbra smiled. "He has conquered the darkness in his heart and obtained the shadow element."

With the final element, his chainmail armor became a red with purple trimmings as the orb that he pulled when his trial began had finally taken the shape of a greatsword.

"Such a remarkable greatsword you have there! What is its name?"

"Ignis." Magnetin swung his sword around to get a feel for his new weapon, it moved swiftly in the air.

"Let me be the first to congratulate you on becoming a full-fledged Dragon Knight," Umbra said with sincerity. "To be honest, I thought you were gonna give up at times."

"I'm happy for you, Magnetin," Vaniglia said with glee. Her ghost began to fade a bit. "Oh, I guess it's time for me to go."

"Vaniglia…" Magnetin turned and closed his eyes. "I'm glad I got to see you one last time. Thank you."

"Arrivederci, Magnetin Darkwind." And with that, Vaniglia returned to the afterlife.

"We should return to the Realm of the Living," Umbra suggested.

"Right."

EPILOGUE

The Weak and the Strong

It has gotten dark since Magnetin has entered the catacombs. Francis couldn't help but let out a deep yawn. Seeing this caused Cinghiale to yawn as well as the two went back and forth.

Delphine couldn't help but yawn as well after watching the two constantly. "Stop that! It's contagious!"

"How much longer is this gonna take?" Anita asked Kamori.

"It depends. Hopefully not too much longer."

"I hope so. I wanna get some sleep." Cinghiale yawned again.

"I want some action. We've been sitting on the sidelines, watching Magnetin have all the action." Francis was frustrated with nothing to do.

Lyndis looked up at the sky and saw something peculiar. "You might get your wish tonight: The moon is full."

"The full moon is where Wraith's influence is at its strongest." Draco saw the warning signs. Before they knew it, they saw hundreds of lit torches moving in the distance. It was all of the villagers, young and old, marching through towards them. There were about ten thousand, give or take. "Yep, this is the extent of it."

"Oh, shit…" Cinghiale cursed at their luck.

"What are we gonna do? There are way too many!" The villagers surrounded the old courtyard, preventing escape. Although the enemy is a group of untrained humans, the sheer numbers could prove unbearable.

"Well, I don't know about you, but I don't want to be served over a fire!" Cinghiale took up his brawler stance.

"And I ain't running with my tail between my legs anymore!" Francis agreed with the brawler for once. Everyone split up and took on a set number of villagers, but all of them were soon faced, back-to-back, completely surrounded outside the courtyards on all sides.

"Something's wrong with these humans! My shots keep missing!"

"Wraith is using illusions to cloud our vision!"

Suddenly, the ground began to shake violently as they saw someone jump high into the air, wielding a giant hammer and striking down on the ground hard, causing a number of humans to fly into the air on impact.

"Oh, your majesty!" Delphine saw that it was Queen Johanna.

"I heard from Umbra. It appears I made it just in time, and I am not alone!" Indeed, she wasn't, as ten of her entire royal guard followed as well as several of Maritian Warriors.

"Why it's Esk, too!" Anita was surprised by this change of events.

"Fight on, brethren! Maul them!" Esk commanded his fellow Maritians to fight, in his hand was the staff Zero Celsius left behind.

There was also chanting heard near the mountain ridge. It was Van'jin and ten of the Moltenstone Trolls who were all coming down from their mountain to lend a hand. In her hand was Cinder Lavaguard's spear. "No one be harmin' anyone, so long as me and me tribe can say about it!" Now they stood a fighting chance as the numbers evened out slightly. But the result didn't change.

"Man, this Wraith is cheating, isn't it!?" Francis growled. "Damn that parasite!"

"It's the moon! As long as the moonlight is shining down on them, we cannot strike them." Kamori informed them, flying high to avoid several of the "children" trying to grab him.

"Then how's about we cut their source of power?" A voice was heard from within the castle, causing all heads to turn. Magnetin had stepped out into the open.

"It's the fucking lizard…"

"That's PRINCE Darkwind to you, human!" Magnetin retorted.

"Magnetin! You've done it!" Lyndis was more than happy to see him a full-fledged Dragon Knight. Everyone, especially Queen Johanna and the royal guards, was surprised and happy for Magnetin. Behind him was Umbra Cryptlurker.

"Umbra?" Magnetin addressed her. "Care to do the honors?"

"With pleasure." The Guardian of Shadows began to draw the area into the Shadow Realm, completely blocking the moon from vision. "Welcome to my realm! The Shadow Realm!"

"Our chance is now! Kill them all!" Draco saw the opportunity at hand as he severed the bodies of two humans in half, one male and one female. "Make sure none are spared!"

"Are you sure!?" Delphine said with concern.

"They are consumed by the madness of Wraith! We have no other choice!" The mad villagers began to panic and tried to flee. Everyone began to execute each and every villager in order to prevent Wraith's influence on them from escaping. Some, like Lyndis, made their deaths as quick and painless as possible, while others, like Francis, who was still furious at the mad villagers, killed all those unfortunate enough as brutally and savagely as possible. Umbra was having fun toying with some of the mad villagers. The soldiers all kept the villagers from escaping their fate. During the battle, Delphine went over to a nearby lake and purified the water so they could cleanse the bodies of the villagers of Wraith once they were executed. However, the influence was so great that it slowly dissolved their bodies completely, including their bones.

While Magnetin was slaying the mad villagers, he came across a familiar face. "You…" It was the very same man who killed Vaniglia. Magnetin grabbed the man by the shirt collar back, pulling him closer, having a serious bone to pick with him. "We finally meet again after all these years! And this time the tables have turned!" The human tried to punch Magnetin in the face, but to no effect. Magnetin then punched the man several times in the face. "Look, you fucking human, see what you have done!? All this is YOUR fault!" Magnetin took all of the words this man said to him in the past and forcing him to witness and feel the consequences in full effect. Magnetin then released the man and sliced his body in two with one swift horizontal motion, heating his greatsword to where he was able to sever the flesh and bones like a hot knife through butter. "Don't worry, I have put you out of your misery!"

After several moments, they've finished slaying the rest of the villagers and now their bodies are being thrown into the pool of holy water to be cleansed.

"That was fun…" Delphine said, sarcastically. She takes no pleasure in killing others. "Hope I never have to do that again…"

"Indeed." Queen Johanna agreed somewhat. "I'm just glad this horrible deed is over with." Magnetin stood in his Dragon Knight armor. "You've finally done it, my heir."

"We're not done yet, are we?" Magnetin asked his grandmother. Queen Johanna just shook her head. "Right." Magnetin walked around in search of something until he came to a spot he recognized. This was the spot that Vaniglia died and was buried. The grave was surrounded by gemstones. Magnetin had drawn the sword that was slain her, he wrapped up the blade together earlier since it was broken and stabbed it into the ground. Delphine had approached Magnetin and saw him walk away from Vaniglia's grave. She looked concerned until the ghost of Vaniglia loomed over her grave.

"Hello, Miss Delphine Lightwind." Vaniglia gained Delphine's attention. "I want to thank you for all that you have done for Magnetin."

"You are?"

"My name is Vaniglia, I was an acolyte of Stonworth Castle and Magnetin's caretaker. I, unfortunately, had died in my duty and it traumatized him greatly. But now, thanks to you and your friends, he's now free. Please, continue to watch over him for me in my place."

"It'll be my honor." Delphine bowed in respect. She then turned to Magnetin walking away as Vaniglia's ghost vanished again.

Whatever happens from here on out.
My pain shall make me stronger.

The weak become strong, I'll become stronger!

To be continued…